D1395140

PB B

CLASS	A F	L......
AUTHOR		

'Hey, pumpkin, Alexandra's going to sit with you while Daddy's having a wash. Is that okay?'

Big brown eyes impaled Alex, full of caution but also recognition. 'Okay.'

Alex felt as though she'd been bestowed with a huge honour. 'I've got a story to read you. Do you like dogs, Sophia?'

The little head dipped in acknowledgement.

Alex settled closer and, bending her head nearer Sophia, began to read.

I could get to enjoy this. The book shook in her hands; her voice wobbled. *I could? Darned right, I could.*

Mario's feet were glued to the floor. He knew he should be grabbing the opportunity to shower and put on clean clothes, but he was riveted to the sight of Sophia snuggling up to Alexandra.

Dear Reader

I'm often asked where the ideas for my stories come from, and I have to say I haven't got a clue. They just arrive in my head. Yes, it's chaos in there sometimes.

So where did Mario and Alexandra come from? In the sunshine by the marina at a restaurant in Nelson, celebrating a friend's birthday earlier this year, I found my story. Sitting at another table was a very big, gorgeous, Italian-looking guy.

And that's how it began. What if this man was a doctor? What if he was bringing up a child alone? Why? What kind of woman would take his heart? It was easy to visualise a tiny but strong woman with him. And how perfect it would be to make her his boss.

We had a great lunch that day, and I didn't spend all my time on the story, preferring to enjoy the celebrations. But during the hour and a half drive home my mind worked overtime. I hope you like the result.

Cheers!

Sue MacKay

www.suemackay.co.nz

sue.mackay56@yahoo.com

YOU, ME AND A FAMILY

BY
SUE MacKAY

STIRLING
COUNCIL
LIBRARIES

All the characters in this book have no existence outside the imagination of the author, and have no relation whatsoever to anyone bearing the same name or names. They are not even distantly inspired by any individual known or unknown to the author, and all the incidents are pure invention.

All Rights Reserved including the right of reproduction in whole or in part in any form. This edition is published by arrangement with Harlequin Enterprises II BV/S.à.r.l. The text of this publication or any part thereof may not be reproduced or transmitted in any form or by any means, electronic or mechanical, including photocopying, recording, storage in an information retrieval system, or otherwise, without the written permission of the publisher.

® and TM are trademarks owned and used by the trademark owner and/or its licensee. Trademarks marked with ® are registered with the United Kingdom Patent Office and/or the Office for Harmonisation in the Internal Market and in other countries.

First published in Great Britain 2013
by Mills & Boon, an imprint of Harlequin (UK) Limited.
Large Print edition 2013
Harlequin (UK) Limited, Eton House,
18-24 Paradise Road, Richmond, Surrey TW9 1SR

© Sue MacKay 2013

ISBN: 978 0 263 23136 6

Harlequin (UK) policy is to use papers that are natural, renewable and recyclable products and made from wood grown in sustainable forests. The logging and manufacturing process conform to the legal environmental regulations of the country of origin.

Printed and bound in Great Britain
by CPI Antony Rowe, Chippenham, Wiltshire

With a background of working in medical laboratories and a love of the romance genre, it is no surprise that **Sue MacKay** writes Mills & Boon® Medical Romance™ stories. An avid reader all her life, she wrote her first story at age eight—about a prince, of course. She lives with her own hero in the beautiful Marlborough Sounds, at the top of New Zealand's South Island, where she indulges her passions for the outdoors, the sea and cycling.

To Dad and Mum

No matter what, you were always there for us as we grew from little hellions to adults.

I miss you.

Also by Sue MacKay:

CHRISTMAS WITH DR DELICIOUS
EVERY BOY'S DREAM DAD
THE DANGERS OF DATING YOUR BOSS
SURGEON IN A WEDDING DRESS
RETURN OF THE MAVERICK
PLAYBOY DOCTOR TO DOTING DAD
THEIR MARRIAGE MIRACLE

**These books are also available in eBook format
from www.millsandboon.co.uk**

CHAPTER ONE

'ALEXANDRA KATHERINE PRENDERGAST, how do you plead? Guilty…?'

The judge paused, drawing out the excruciating moment, forcing her heart to clench with pain.

Just when Alex thought she'd scream with frustration and humiliation, he added in a disbelieving taunt, 'Or not guilty?'

Her mouth was drier than a hot summer's day. Her tongue felt twice its normal size. Tears oozed from the corners of her eyes to track down her sallow cheeks. 'Guilty,' she tried to whisper. *Guilty, guilty, guilty,* cried her brain, agreed her knotted belly.

'Speak up, Alexandra,' the man standing on the opposite side of the operating theatre table growled. His eyes, staring out at her from under his cap, were cold, hard and demanding. Their hue matched the no-nonsense blue of the scrubs they both wore. 'Did this child die in your care or not?'

'I did everything within my power to keep him alive, your honour. The other doctors told me there was nothing I could've done, that I did nothing wrong. I wanted to believe them, but how could I? He was totally reliant on me and I failed him.' The familiar, gut-twisting mantra spilled over her sore, cracked lips. The old pain and despair roiled up her throat. 'I failed Jordan.' The words flailed her brain.

'Jordan died because of you. Have you done everything within your power to prevent the same thing happening again?'

'Yes,' she croaked. 'Every day I try to save other babies.'

'I sentence you to a lifetime of looking after other people's ill children.' Her judge's eyes were icy, his voice a perfect match.

Alex gasped, shoved up from her pillow and clamped her hand over her mouth. Sweat soaked her nightgown, plastering it to her breasts and shoulders, making it pull tight against her skin as she moved in the bed. Moist strands of hair fell into her eyes, stuck to her wet cheeks. 'I will not throw up. I will not.' The words stuck in the back of her throat as she blinked her way back from the nightmare.

The all too familiar nightmare.

Her fingers shook as she reached for the bedside lamp switch and flooded her bedroom with soft yellow light. Tossing the covers aside she put her feet on the floor and pushed up. Despite the heat-pump being on, the winter air was chilly on her feverish skin. But cold was good. It focused her. Brought her completely back from the nightmare and her guilt. Made her concentrate on the here and now, on today and not the past.

Tugging on a thick robe and slipping her feet into fluffy slippers she trudged out to the kitchen and plugged the kettle in to make a drink of herbal tea. Shivering, she stood staring into her pantry, unable to decide what flavour to have. Her eyes welled up as the floodgates opened, and she blindly reached for the nearest packet and plopped a tea bag into a mug.

The oven clock read 3:46. She'd had little more than three hours sleep before the nightmare hit, slamming into her head in full technicolour. Accusing. Debilitating. Painful. Reminding her that her position as head paediatrician at Nelson Hospital was, in her mind, as tenuous as whatever her next patient threw at her. Taunting she was a fraud and that it was only a matter of time before she made a dreadful mistake with someone's child that would expose her as incompetent.

She had to draw deep to find the belief she was a good doctor, a very good one. The ever expanding numbers of sick children coming to see her, not just from the top of the South Island but all over New Zealand, showed that. Unfortunately the nightmare always undermined her fragile belief in herself.

It also reinforced the truth about her not being mother material, how totally incompetent she'd be in that role. Not that she'd be contemplating that ever again.

Click. The kettle switched off. Boiling water splashed onto the counter as she filled her mug. Strawberry vapour rose to her nostrils. Taking the drink she crossed through the lounge to the wide, floor-to-ceiling window showcasing the lights of Rocks Road and the wharves of Nelson Harbour. Rain slashed through the night, falling in sheets to puddle on the surface ten storeys below.

Alex stood, shaking, clutching the hot mug in both hands, and staring down at the tugboats manoeuvring a freight ship through the narrow cut leading from Tasman Bay to the sheltered harbour. Day and night, boats came and went according to the tides. Now, in early June, they'd be loading the last of the kiwifruit destined for the other side of the world. Men looking like midgets worked ropes and machinery. A tough job. An honest job.

'Stop it.' There was nothing easy or dishonest about the work she did with sick children. 'You did not cause Jordan's death. The pathologist proved that, exonerated you.'

Tell that to Jordan's father.

Behind her eyes a steady pounding built in intensity. Alex cautiously sipped the steaming tea, her gaze still fixed on the wet scene below. Why had the nightmares returned tonight? Exhaustion? Or the nagging need to slot back into her role as head of paediatrics at Nelson Hospital as quickly and effortlessly as possible?

The job was more than a job—it was her whole life, a replacement for the family she wouldn't otherwise have. Lots of staff to mentor, harangue, watch over and care about. Oodles of children to care for in the only way she knew how—medically—and to love safely from the sidelines. Involved, yet not involved.

The fruity scent of her tea wafted in the air, sweet and relaxing. 'You shouldn't have taken the four-month sabbatical. It put you under pressure to again prove how good you are.'

But all those American hospitals and their savvy specialists showing how brilliant they were had actually boosted her confidence and made her understand once and for all she was up with the play, had joined the ranks of the best in the business of paediatrics. Everywhere she'd gone she'd been applauded for her paper on premature births. The job offers had been overwhelming. An awesome charge for her fragile ego. Even the nagging need to constantly prove to herself that she was good had taken a hike.

In San Francisco, when her old mentor from specialising days had offered her an incredible position at his new private paediatric clinic, she'd been beside herself with pride.

And that, she thought with grim satisfaction, should earn her stepfather's grudging respect. Except, of course, she'd turned it down.

Draining the mug Alex turned away from the window. Time to try for some more sleep. Jet lag, exhaustion from her hectic time in the States, the inability to relax while away from home. All reasons to explain why she ached with tiredness and her mind ran riot with yearnings for what seemed doomed forever. A family of her own to love and cherish.

Alexandra sighed through her throbbing headache as she dropped her handbag into the bottom drawer of her desk. Home, sweet home. Nelson Hospital Paediatric Department. The place she spent most of her life. Her stomach flip-flopped like a fish on dry sand. Nerves? Why? She was happy to be back. Wasn't she? Yes, but what if there'd been too many changes on the ward in her absence? Which regular patients had got well and left? Had any of them passed away?

She shivered. What was wrong with her this morning? To be feeling out of sorts was not the best way to start back on the job.

She'd been determined not to think too much about this job while she'd studied with the best of paediatricians in California and Washington, or when she'd presented her paper to countless meetings and conventions. During that time she'd pretended she wasn't worried about staffing levels and the ever increasing numbers of wee patients entering Nelson Hospital. Instead she'd tried to absorb all she could from her mentors and share her own experiences and knowledge. She'd been entertained, courted and tutored. And all she'd wanted to do was return here. Home. Where she felt safe.

She glanced around the familiar room at the paintings she'd bought at the annual summer art show in the Queen's Gardens downtown. They looked tired. Like her. Dusty. Not like her. She smiled reluctantly. It was great to be back—dust, or no dust.

Then reality crashed in on her. Her desk should be littered with stacks of files, notes, memos and all the other detritus that accumulated on a daily basis. Instead there was one small, neat pile in the centre of her desk. The acting HOD from London must've decided to give her a break on her first day back, despite having warned her during their Skype interview he'd be a better doctor than pen-pusher. 'Thanks, John. I owe you.'

Stepping closer she spied a note at the top of the pile and picked it up.

Miss Alexandra Prendergast. Welcome back. I've done the rosters for the next month, signed off the patient reports to date and answered all the mail apart from two letters regarding intern rotations you might like to deal with yourself. I hope you find everything in order.

The scrawled signature read something like Maria Forreel.

Who was Maria Forreel? And why was this woman working in her office? So much for thinking John had done all this. Forreel? What kind of name was that? Was it—? Her smile stretched into a grin. Seriously, was it for real? Alex peered closer. Forell? Forelli, that was it. Forelli. It made no difference. The name meant nothing to her.

Alex tugged the chair out from the desk and sank down on it. She had been excited about coming back and yet today felt like the first day at school—terrifying. Worse, she didn't even know why. 'Probably jet lag.' How many things could she blame on that?

'There you are. How was your trip? Did you do lots of shopping in all those swanky boutiques?' The charge nurse on her ward stood in the doorway with a wide, welcoming smile on her dear face.

'Kay, it's great to see you.' A welcome distraction. 'And yes, I found time to add to my wardrobe. A lot.'

'I'm so-o jealous.' Kay gave the most unjealous grin possible.

Alex reached into the drawer where she'd placed her handbag and pulled out a small package. 'I hope you like these.'

Kay gaped. 'You bought me something? Oh, you big softy. What is it?' The paper tore under her fingers. 'Oh, my gosh. They're beautiful.' She held up the silver earrings, turning them left and right so the light gleamed off the polished metal. 'I love them. Thank you so much. But you shouldn't have.'

Alex laughed. 'Of course I shouldn't. You'll have to work twice as hard now.' Like Kay could do that. She was already the hardest working nurse Alex had ever come across. She added, 'I'm glad you like them. When I saw them I immediately thought of you.' She had little trinkets for the rest of the staff too.

Kay slipped the hooks into her ears. 'Where's a mirror?' She took the one Alex handed her from the drawer. 'Wow, they're perfect.'

Alex rose, smoothed the skirt of her tailored suit and reached for her white coat hanging on the back of the door. 'So how's Darren? The kids?'

'Busy as ever. Why didn't I appreciate my single, peaceful life when I had it?' Kay grinned again.

'You wouldn't swap a thing.' *Whereas I would*

swap my amazing medical career for exactly what Kay's got. Alex gulped. Her fingers faltered on the buttons they were doing up. What? *I'd love a Darren and some kids in my life? Okay, not exactly Darren but a loving, caring man who'd understand my eccentricities and forgive me my mistakes in a flash. I would? Since when?* Under her ribs her heart beat a heavy rhythm. Her shoulders drooped momentarily. As if a man like that existed for her. Pressing her fingers to her temples she breathed in slowly. This day was going all weird on her and it was only seven in the morning. Things had better start looking up soon.

'Alex? Are you all right?' Kay was at her elbow, her brow creased with concern.

'I'm fine.' She dropped her hands.

'Are you sure you should be starting back today? You only got back into the country yesterday, didn't you?'

Kay's concern would be her undoing if she let it. 'I'm fine. Raring to go, in fact.' Alex hauled her shoulders back into place and plastered a tight smile on her face, then reminded herself where

she was. At work, in her comfort zone. She relaxed. A little. 'I'm a bit tired, nothing else. Rushing from one city to the next took its toll.'

Kay gave an exaggerated eye roll. 'My heart
bleeds for you.'

Alex laughed, finally feeling secure with being
back at work. Kay always kept her grounded
when the going got rough, and today hadn't even
started. 'I know I'm early but let's get the shift
under way. What's been going on in my absence?'

Instantly Kay's demeanour turned serious.
She pointed to an envelope tucked half under
the files lying on her desk. 'There's a message
you need to deal with before anything else. I believe it explains everything.' She headed for the
door. 'Umm, we've had some changes. Big ones.'
Suddenly Kay was in an awful hurry to be gone.
'Good ones.'

Good changes? What was wrong with how
things were before? She ran a well-organised and
successful department. There wasn't any need to
alter a thing. Her unease increased as she reached
tentatively for the missive. 'Why? Has something
happened?'

Beep, beep. The pager on her desk interrupted. Snatching it up she glanced at the message as she ran out of her office right behind Kay, who was racing for the ward. Then the loudspeaker crackled to life and told them what they needed to know. 'Cardiac arrest, room four.'

'Tommy Jenkins.' Kay shoved the fire door back so hard it hit the wall. 'It's so unfair.'

Alex ducked around the door as it swung back, and kept running. 'Who's Tommy Jenkins? Fill me in. Quickly.'

'He and his mother moved to Nelson to be closer to Tommy's grandparents last month after his father died in a fishing accident. Tommy has cystic fibrosis and was admitted five days ago with a massive chest infection that's not responding to any treatment.'

'What an awful time to shift the boy.'

'Tell me about it.' Kay scowled. 'He's missing his mates, and isn't happy about getting to know new medical staff.'

Room four was chaos. The boy lay with his head tipped back while a nurse, Rochelle, inflated his lungs with an Ambu bag. Jackson, an intern, crouched astride him, doing compressions on his chest.

'Hand me the tube,' a deep male voice Alex had never heard in her life ordered calmly. 'Now, please.'

'Here.' Kay obliged in an instant.

Alex pushed in beside Rochelle, ready to take over. She needed to be in control of this situation. Staring at the stranger, who admittedly seemed to know what he was doing, she demanded, 'Who, may I ask, are you?' He certainly wasn't the man she'd Skyped with about taking her place on the ward. This man she'd never forget. A strong jawline, a mouth that smiled as easily as breathing. Eyes that demanded attention.

'Mario Forelli.' He didn't look up, didn't falter in suctioning the boy's mouth. 'This lad's arrested.'

Since it didn't look like she'd be pushing this man out of the way any time soon and wanting something to do with her hands she reached for the drugs bag. 'What are you doing here?' Alex asked, feeling even more perplexed, while at the same time recognising the name on that note in her office. Not Maria, but Mario. Not a woman, but a well-muscled, broad-chested, dark-haired male.

'Mr Forelli, as in paediatric specialist,' Kay spoke from across the bed where she read the monitor keeping track of Tommy's status.

'Stop the compressions.' The stranger spoke clearly but quietly as he deftly inserted a tube down the boy's throat.

'How long has Tommy been down?' Alex asked while her brain tossed up distracting questions. Where had Mr Forelli come from? More importantly, what was he doing on her ward? And taking care of all her paperwork? Where was John Campbell? Big changes, Kay had said. Presumably this man was one of them. Alex forced herself to concentrate as she drew up the drugs in preparation to inserting them into Tommy's intravenous line. Right now this lad depended on her being focused on him, nothing or anyone else.

This Forelli character had no qualms about taking command as he asked Jackson to move aside so he could resume the chest massage. His hands were ludicrously large against the boy's thin, pale chest. He explained to the room in general, 'I found Tommy lying half out of bed a few minutes ago.'

'I'd popped out to get his meds only moments before.' Guilt laced Rochelle's voice as she glanced at Forelli, a disturbingly ingratiating look in her calf-like eyes.

'You mustn't blame yourself, Rochelle. No one could've predicted he'd go into cardiac arrest at that moment.'

Relief poured through the young nurse. 'Thank you, Mario,' she murmured.

Blimey. 'Just as well you were here, Mr Forelli,' Alex muttered, trying to ignore the flare of anger that there was a new doctor on *her* ward whom she knew nothing about. What was the point of being head of department if no one consulted her about something this important? Even if she hadn't been here, someone could've mentioned it in one of the many emails she'd been sent throughout her trip, supposedly keeping her up to date with staff gossip and scandal. She'd have preferred knowing about Forelli's arrival than Rochelle's cousin's car accident.

Forelli gave a quick flick of his dark head in her direction, a beautiful, winsome smile lightening a seriously good-looking face. 'You must be the marvellous Miss Prendergast I've been hearing so much about.' There'd been no change in the rhythm of the compressions. Very smooth.

'I am,' she retorted. *Think you can charm me? Think again, buster.* So why the flutter in her tummy? Why the sense of something she couldn't quite fathom slipping past her fingertips? Her reaction had nothing to do with that sexy voice with a hint of an accent that made her melt inside. No, it had to be the fear of them losing Tommy. There was so much she needed to find out about.

After they'd saved the boy. According to the notes Tommy was fourteen years old. Too young to be in this situation. He hadn't even begun to experience life, and if his heart didn't start soon he'd never get the chance.

Squashing the distress flaring within her she focused on the monitors and pleaded for Tommy's weary heart to start pumping, itching to take over the compressions, feeling ridiculously useless as everyone worked well together.

The room went quiet as everyone concentrated on bringing Tommy back to life. More compressions, drugs and oxygen. Finally, Forelli sucked a lungful and commanded, 'Stop.' Everyone held their breath and watched the monitor's screen.

At last a rhythm appeared. A collective sigh of relief and a thankful 'Yes' resounded around the small room.

Alex fought to keep her shoulders from slumping. That had been too close. 'Is Tommy's mother in the hospital?' she asked Kay after she'd administered another dose of adrenaline.

'No. She usually comes in about nine and spends an hour or two with Tommy before going back home to work. She's still got her old job, working online. A tax lawyer for the government, I think. I'll phone her to come in early.'

'Thanks, Kay. I'll talk to Mrs Jenkins when she gets in. In the meantime I'd like to be brought up to date on everyone else on the ward.' Her eyes clashed with Forelli's pewter-coloured gaze. 'That includes you.'

He shrugged eloquently. 'No problem.'

'We'll talk after I've spoken to whoever's in charge of Tommy's case.'

Those eyes twinkled at her. 'That would be me. I've been taking care of this young man since he was admitted for the first time a month ago.' Before she knew what was happening Forelli put out his right hand to engulf hers in a warm, firm grip. 'We haven't had a chance to meet properly. Mario Forelli. Your new paediatrician.' He shook her hand, but didn't immediately let her go, holding her hand in an almost caress.

'Excuse me?' She tugged free, trying to ignore the spear of warmth zooming up her arm. 'Do you mind telling me how you fit in here?' Talk about being on the back foot in her own department.

'Certainly. Shall we each grab a coffee and go to your office, maybe after I've talked to Carla Jenkins?'

Her eyes locked on to Mario Forelli. Another charmer. The world seemed full of them. And yet his return gaze showed understanding and commiseration at her situation. Which rattled her further, cranking her stress levels dangerously high. Breathe deep, one, two, three. 'Thank you. I'd appreciate it.'

She headed for the nurses' station. Mr Forelli strode alongside her, towering above her, making her feel even shorter than usual. Strangely, that didn't bother her the way it usually did. Who was this guy? How did he so easily get under her skin? She spun around to get a better look at him and tripped over her own feet. She would've fallen flat on her face if *he* hadn't caught her elbow.

'Careful.'

'Thanks.' Again. Alex glared up at this disturbing man, and stretched onto the toes of her new Italian shoes from Los Angeles. Still way too short for level eye contact. For that she'd need a small ladder. Grr.

'Mario, can I get your signature on this letter?' Averill, Alex's secretary, stood in front of them, a dazzling smile on her face as she peered up at Mario.

'Sure.' He reached for the pad and pen being held out to him.

'Ah, hum. Excuse me.' Alex looked from Averill to Mario.

Her secretary finally dragged her eyes sideways and recognised Alex. 'Hi, Alex, you're back.'

'Yes, I'm back.' Since when did Averill come in so early? The starstruck look on the older woman's face held the answer. Since Mr Forelli had started working here. Alex continued watching the pair of them but had to admit the new doctor wasn't encouraging Averill in any way whatsoever.

Mario handed the pen and memo back, his signature scrawled across the bottom. 'There you go.'

As her secretary scuttled away Alex damped down the sudden fear brought on by her own stupid insecurities and rounded on Mr Forelli to demand some answers. The words dried on her tongue when her eyes clashed with his.

'Averill wasn't going over your head to get me to sign that. It was a letter from me to the board about my tenure.' When she again tried to speak he held his hand up. 'We'll talk as soon as we get our patients sorted. Okay?'

'Oh, fine, thanks.' What was she thanking him for? Flustered she looked away. If she went home and started her day again would it get any better? Another glance in his direction didn't clear anything up. Instead his open face and friendly eyes beguiled her. And his practical approach undermined her concerns, told her she had nothing to worry about.

'One hour.' He waved at her as he headed down the ward. 'Hopefully.'

Did she mention how he stole her breath away?

Kay stopped on her way past and joined her in watching Forelli's progress down the ward. 'Delectable, don't you think?'

'No, I don't.' *He's the most beautiful man I've ever met. Just standing in front of him makes me feel tiny and delicate.*

'You're the only woman on the ward to think so. He's charmed every female within miles.' Kay chuckled. 'He's got the staff falling over one another to help him out.'

Why am I not surprised? Those smiles alone would get him anything he wanted. But not from her. No, she was here to work, not play. Disappointment flared. Playing with Mr Forelli after hours might be fun, exciting even. 'How long's he been working here?'

When her head nurse didn't answer Alex turned around to see Kay quickly disappearing behind the nurses' station, her gaze intent on the file in her hand. Right. Alex followed, wondering how she could wait a whole hour to learn more about Mr Forelli.

Suddenly it dawned on her she was letting everything get out of control. She still hadn't caught up on the patients. Mr Forelli's presence had knocked her sideways. Since when did she let these things faze her? *Come on. You worry too much. There were bound to be some changes made during your absence. Hospitals don't stand still.*

Little more than one hour back on the ward and she was shattered. And she'd thought touring was hard work.

'Welcome home, Alex,' she muttered. Would anyone notice if she walked away, grabbed a flight to anywhere and buried her head in the clouds for another day? Probably not if what she'd seen of Mr Forelli was anything to go by. He was definitely in charge—of her department.

CHAPTER TWO

'SO THAT'S THE wonderful Miss Prendergast.'
Mario's hands clenched and unclenched at his
sides. Imperious despite being as confused as all
be it. Did she honestly think the whole ward had
been waiting, going nowhere, achieving nothing,
until she returned to the helm?

She hadn't exactly rushed him with her enthusiasm at his presence. What she had done was
disturb him deep inside where he hid his emotions. Right now that pool of feelings was swirl-
ing, putting him on high alert. If she could do this
to him in such a short time she was dangerous to
his equilibrium. Very dangerous. He needed to
exercise caution. But how when just being near
all that loveliness tied up in a mouth-watering
package made him feel drunk. She was a neat
package that reminded him of what he'd been

missing out on for nearly a year, and what he did not have the time for now—a sex life.

His teeth ground hard as he cursed under his breath. He really enjoyed this job, but today it was shaping up to be a pain in the butt. Or a tickle in his hormone department.

Worse, like an ungainly teen, he'd struggled to stop ogling at her exquisite features: high cheekbones, pert nose, flawless skin. Not to mention that gleaming auburn hair locked up in a knot so tight not one strand could escape. 'She's so tiny. Yet her reputation is huge.' A powerhouse on heels.

As he continued to study her it dawned on him that he'd been expecting an Amazon woman to match the stories he'd heard about her—a demanding, punishing doctor who expected unsurpassed devotion towards the patients from each and every member of her staff, who accepted nothing but the finest care and treatment for every child entering this ward, and would do whatever it took to get it. Including, so he'd been told, reading stories to wee tots at all hours of the night and day. So he had that much in common with her. He'd also heard she cared a lot for her staff.

Those amazing green eyes, filled with angry questions, had sizzled at him, bursting with frustration because she didn't know what was going on in her domain. Never mind she'd been away a third of the year. Admittedly he fully understood her feelings. He'd be the same in a similar situation. *Scema.*

He'd expected it. Even in Italy he'd heard of Alexandra Prendergast and her groundbreaking theories on dealing with premature infants. He'd read the paper she'd written and had been keen to meet her, to work with her. Who hadn't?

Why hadn't she taken up a grand position in a large hospital overseas? Mistakes in her past? Something had rattled her in Tommy's room. There'd been a fear lurking in her eyes until the boy's heart restarted. Whatever caused it had tugged at his heartstrings, had made him want to wrap her up in a hug and protect her. As if she'd let him even try. As if he had time for another female, another broken soul, to look out for.

Because right now his focus had to be totally

on Sophia. Which left no room in his life for anything, anyone, else. Sophia ruled everything including his heart. Getting his wee daughter's life back on track, making her happy and, hopefully, finally winning spontaneous smiles from her sweet cupid's mouth was paramount. Everything else was on hold for as long as it took and beyond.

He shrugged. Enough conjecturing. His first move would be to explain his presence without going into any personal details. Was it too much to hope she wouldn't notice the six-month gap in his CV? The CV the board's chairman insisted he show Alexandra, even though the job was his. Maybe he could forestall too many questions by talking about the reason for Liz's abrupt departure from the department.

Sighing, Mario finally managed to stop staring and instead called to her. 'Do you want to join me when I talk to Carla Jenkins?'

Her eyes lightened and that tautness in her shoulders relaxed. 'Yes. I should meet her.'

Just then a distressed woman in her thirties burst out of the lift and shot straight towards him, tears streaming down her cheeks. 'Mario, what's happened? Is Tommy all right?' Carla rushed at him. 'Kay told me to come in immediately. What's wrong?'

Mario looked into Carla's imploring eyes and had one of those moments when he hated his job. He understood her fears. Really understood them. He'd be absolutely terrified if Sophia's heart had stopped. 'Tommy's fine now but his heart stopped for a while.' He paused to let his words sink in. When Carla's eyes widened and her bottom lip trembled, he pressed her shoulder gently, and repeated, 'He's all right now.'

'I have to see him.' Fear and despair laced Carla's voice. 'I shouldn't have moved here, but it was so hard dealing with this on my own after everything else.'

'Tommy's no worse off being here. His heart would've stopped if he'd been in Auckland.' Taking Carla's elbow Mario gently led her into a visitors' room. 'The nurses are staying with him and you can see him once I've explained what happened.'

Alexandra followed and shut the door firmly.

Then she reiterated his first statement. 'Tommy's heart is beating fine now.'

'Who are you? Why did it stop? Are you sure he's all right?' Carla stopped the torrent of words and swallowed hard. Tears gleamed at the corners of her eyes as she stared at the door as though wishing Tommy would walk through and hug her. Her fingers were tightly interlaced against her stomach, her elbows taut and awkward at her sides. 'Sorry. I freaked when Kay phoned.'

'Take a seat, Carla.' Mario parked his backside on the edge of the small table. 'This is Miss Prendergast. You've heard about her and she'll be part of Tommy's medical team from now on. She's very experienced and Tommy couldn't be in better hands.' Hell, Tommy was getting excellent care in *his* hands.

Glancing around, he found Alexandra's eyebrows lifting ever so slightly as she listened to him, amusement blinking back at him from those emerald eyes. Had he gone overboard with his compliment? With a shrug, he got back to the main reason they were all shut in this airless room. 'Do you recall the conversation you and

I had when Tommy was first admitted? About what to expect at this stage of Tommy's disease?'

'Yes, but I hoped you were wrong. No, I prayed you didn't know what you were talking about. They didn't put it so bluntly in Auckland. I'm sorry.' Carla sagged further.

Mario winced. There was nothing to be gained by keeping a patient's family in the dark. But then Carla and her son had been dealing with another tragedy, and anything else might've overwhelmed them at the time.

Alexandra took the empty seat beside the woman and reached for Carla's hands. So here was Miss Prendergast's softer side. 'It's very understandable for you to hope for better. I'd probably do the same thing if I was in your situation.' She shook Carla's hands gently. 'But as doctors we don't have that luxury. We have to be prepared for anything to happen so that we can do our very best for Tommy.'

Carla lifted her pain-filled eyes to Alexandra's face. 'Thank you.'

Mario watched as Alexandra talked softly, explaining the situation once again, having gone from confused to kind and compassionate in a flash. Amazing how her own priorities had been put aside for a suffering parent. He was impressed. This was the soft caramel specialist he'd heard about.

Alexandra said to Carla, 'What you can keep believing is that we're doing everything possible for Tommy.'

Carla's bottom lip trembled but she blinked hard and held herself very straight. 'I do, but I'm afraid of losing him.'

Mario murmured, '*Sì*. It is very hard for you. But Tommy's fighting hard. He won't give in. I've seen it in his eyes.'

He noted Alexandra listening as carefully as Carla. Sussing him out? Making sure he was up to speed on the job? That rankled. He'd worked in some of the best hospitals in England and Italy. He had an excellent reputation as a surgeon for the little ones. This hospital board had been more than happy to accept his qualifications. Miss Prendergast had to accept him, like it or not. Starting now.

He stood abruptly. The desperate need in

Carla's eyes to see her son gave him the perfect excuse to cut this conversation short. Carla probably couldn't take in any more right now anyway. Taking her elbow he said, 'Come. We'll visit your son.'

He accompanied the woman to Tommy's room where he spent time checking the boy over again. Finally he stepped back and left Carla gripping Tommy's hand and talking soothing mother things while watching her precious son as though he was about to vaporise into thin air.

His heart stuttered. Sophia's mother had never been there for her child. Too busy having a good time to want to be tied down by her daughter. How the hell had she not loved sweet, lovable Sophia? What he wouldn't do to tell Lucy exactly what he thought of her.

As a father he connected with Carla's emotions. The two times Sophia had been severely ill he'd taken her hands in his and hung on for dear life, willing his own life source into her, urging her to come back to him. It had drained him completely, taken days to recover from, but he was her father and fathers gave their all to their bambinos. So should all mothers.

'Have you got time to join me on the ward round?' Alexandra spoke quietly from beside him. 'Or do you want to stay with those two a while longer? I don't mind waiting if you do.'

When he turned his head and looked down he met the direct but empathetic gaze of this enigmatic woman. 'They don't need me at the moment. Probably better off having time alone. Let's go over patient notes in Kay's cubbyhole she proudly calls her office. I'll bring you up to speed.'

'Right.'

Right. That's it? Did that mean she was accepting his presence? Did she realise he'd been doing her job while she was away? Not to mention filling in for Liz. 'Right,' he snapped back, suddenly tired of this, wanting to clear the air between them now, not after they'd completed their round. But the interns were waiting, grouped around the nurses' station, reading notes, and pestering the nurses. His teeth ground on a curse. He'd have to wait.

At Kay's door he stood back to allow Alexandra to enter first, and as she passed he drew a lungful of sweet spring air that reminded him of freesias. On a freezing winter's day? What was wrong with him? It was as though his brain had gone to hell in a wheelbarrow, leaving him delusional. It certainly wasn't because he was attracted to this woman. Absolutely not. He liked his women pliable and fun, not to mention tall and blonde. Fun especially didn't seem to fit Alexandra. Maybe he could show her some? Bah! Dumb idea. Perturbed at the direction his thoughts were heading he studied Alexandra from behind.

The shapeless white coat did not enhance her figure, but neither did it detract from her attributes. Her slim neck and cute ears poking from above the crinkled white collar appeared delicate. Nothing like the real Miss Prendergast at all.

'Hi, Mario. How's Sophia this morning?' Kay grinned at him.

'As quiet and good as ever.' Sadness struck as he thought of his daughter and her fear of doing something naughty. At times he almost wished she'd throw a tantrum or refuse to do what he asked of her, instead of her quiet sobs in the night and her need to behave perfectly so no one would growl at her. It wasn't normal to be so good. He'd probably never know everything that had happened to her before he'd come into her life. And for now it was more important to help her overcome the past, not make an issue of it. The only way he knew how to do that was to provide stability and loads of unconditional love, things she'd never experienced in her short and sad life.

'I found some of my boys' books and brought them in for Sophia. I hope they're not too young for her but I was thinking that as she's learning to read they'd be a good place to start.'

'I'm sure Sophia will enjoy them. She loves all sorts of books. Just like her dad.' His chest swelled, while at the same time he squashed a pang of annoyance. It was his place to provide everything Sophia needed. If he just had the time to go shopping.

Alexandra's eyes were flicking back and forth between him and Kay, puzzlement darkening the green to the colour of pine needles. 'Sophia's my daughter,' he informed her. Maybe telling her something personal would soften her attitude towards him. 'She's four years old.'

'She's gorgeous,' added Kay, making his heart swell more.

'Of course she's gorgeous.' *She's mine.*

Alexandra's eyes widened but she only said, 'Let's take a look at the patient files, shall we?'

'Sì.' Antagonising this woman wouldn't help anyone, least of all him. He had no intention of finding another specialist position in another city. Nelson was where he belonged, where Sophia now belonged. They were here to stay—forever.

So buying a ticket to Mars was not an option, even if, at this very moment with Alexandra eyeing him up like something the cat had dragged in, all that isolation seemed like bliss.

As Kay handed Alexandra the first file she said in an aside to him, 'I also brought in a chicken casserole for you to take home tonight. I made far too much for us to get through.'

'You're as transparent as glass.' Mario smiled. 'Thank you, but I really wish you wouldn't. I do cook for Sophia every day.' No need to admit that more often than not he heated up something from the freezer, or that often by the time he did have food ready Sophia had fallen asleep on the sofa in front of the TV.

'Just helping you out.' Kay winked, totally unperturbed by his annoyed tone. 'Don't forget to take the dinner home this time.'

Oops. So she'd noticed that the last meal sat in the staff fridge for days before he remembered it was there. Contrite, he smiled. 'I promise I won't.' Quickly scrawling a word on the palm of his hand he shoved his pen back into his pocket and looked up, straight into the amused look on Alexandra's face.

'You don't write memos on your hand?' he asked.

'No, I don't. I have an excellent memory.'

'Unfortunately.' Kay grinned. 'There are times when we all wish you could forget what you've told us to do.'

Startled, Alexandra looked away from this annoying man to gawp at Kay. 'Am I that much of a taskmaster?'

The nurse rolled her eyes and widened her grin. 'The only thing missing is the whip.'

Kay was teasing. Right? A little? What if the staff did think she went too far with her demands of them? 'I can be difficult at times, yes, but I'm only thinking of my patients. I'm not a tyrant. Am I?' She'd been away too long. This was where she faced the world from, wrapping the ward and its inhabitants around her like a security blanket. Now worry gnawed at her. Because she'd found everyone falling over backwards to please Mr Forelli?

Kay chuckled. 'Your little patients adore you, their parents trust you and we all like working here. There, satisfied?'

Mario cleared his throat. 'The patient files?'

The files. Her head jerked up, turning in the direction of that voice that reminded her of red wine and crackers by the fire. Mario Forelli. To be going off on a self-pity tangent was so unlike her. She was tired, and the dregs of her headache still knocked at her skull, but they weren't good enough reasons for this ridiculous behaviour.

Kay tapped her shoulder. 'You're doing it again, going all pale on me.'

'Here.' Warm, strong fingers gripped her elbow, directed her to a chair. 'Take a seat. You must still be jet-lagged. It's a long flight from Los Angeles.' That voice was a balm to her stressed mind, tense muscles.

It also undermined her position as boss. But it was too late to argue. She already sat on the proffered chair. How had she got there so quickly, so effortlessly? Mario Forelli. That's how.

'Thank you. I'm fine, really.' But she stayed seated and reached for the first file. 'Tell me about Gemma Lewis.'

'Gemma has spina bifida. Her family moved here nearly a year ago. Her father is a district court judge. When Gemma required surgery to realign her knees they came to see me rather than return to Wellington.' Forelli's confidence came through loud and clear.

Listening to Forelli explain the surgery he'd performed Alex tried to still the niggling sense of standing on the edge of a precipice. Of falling into a deep chasm she might never find her way

back from. Who was Mario? Other than a paediatrician. In no time at all and with no knowledge of the man her thought processes had been
hijacked in a totally distracting way. Not a good
place to be. Especially, since he had a child, there
was obviously a wife. Or a partner.

Or was he a widower? A million questions
zapped around her skull, cranking up the throbbing behind her eyes. She should've taken a day
at home to fully recover from her trip before facing all these changes.

'Anything you want to ask me about Gemma,
Miss Prendergast?' Mario's voice cut through her
confusion, and focused her on the job.

'I take it that you're a paediatric surgeon, Mr
Forelli.'

His mouth tightened, and she waited for an
angry retort.

He didn't disappoint. 'I am, yes. Which is why
Judge Lewis was comfortable with letting me
look after his daughter.'

'I see.' He hadn't really told her anything but
this wasn't the right arena to be asking with other

staff hanging on to his every word like he was a god.

'The next file is Tommy Jenkins's. You know about him so we'll move on.' He lifted the third file from her fingers. 'Amelia Saunders, ten years old, contracted dengue fever while on holiday in Fiji. Her liver took a pounding but with drugs her LFTs are slowly returning to normal and she's starting to feel a little better. I'm thinking of letting her go home by the end of the week.' The file slapped down on top of Tommy's and another one was tugged from her light grip. 'Andrew Frost. Fractured femur after falling off a horse.' On and on went Mr Forelli. Completely in control. He answered all her questions without hesitation or referring to the patient notes. He knew his stuff. Very impressive.

Finally he said, 'Let's go and see these patients.'

'Of course.' Why was he in such a hurry? Did he want to get the upcoming conversation in her office done and dusted as much as she did? She pushed out of her chair. 'If you'd like to accompany me, Mr Forelli.' And she led the way out the door as Kay's phone rang.

'I'll be right with you,' Kay called after them.

Mario squashed down his annoyance with her. 'Can't you start by calling me Mario?' He gave her a charming grin that defied her to disagree. 'Everyone else does.'

'I think you'll find I'm not everyone else,' she retorted, her proud eyes little warmer than a glacier.

'How true.' He huffed an annoyed breath. 'You're head of paediatrics with a reputation that's the envy of all your peers.' He stopped and leaned oh-so-nonchalantly against the closed doors of the lift access, easing another wide smile across his mouth as he assessed her. Again. What was wrong with him today? Taking all this time to suss out a woman? A woman who clearly didn't want him here. Sure, he was tired after a sleepless night with Sophia but that was nothing new.

Then his mouth got further carried away with, 'You dress superbly.' Any woman would kill for that perfectly fitted navy blue suit and soft draping white blouse.

'Thank you.' Alexandra's tone was still sharp but her eyes were warming. Just.

He started walking. 'How long have you been working in Nelson?' *Where do you live? Who do you live with?*

'Three years.'

'And before that?' *Have you got bambinos running around somewhere? Though if you do, then why aren't you at home with them?* And why did he want to know these things? This was his boss. Her private life was of no interest to him whatsoever. *Just being friendly. And testing the temperature.*

'In San Francisco, specialising.' Alexandra tilted her head so she could glare up at him more thoroughly. 'I'm the one who should be asking questions. Such as, exactly how long have you been working here, Mr Forelli?'

So, not Mario, then. Not yet anyway. But give him time, he'd get there. 'Almost four months.'

Her eyebrows did that imperious rising motion, disappearing under her fringe as the implication of that sunk in. 'Four months?'

'Yes. I started a week after you left for your sabbatical.'

CHAPTER THREE

MARIO STOPPED AT the first door and ushered Alexandra ahead of him. Again freesias teased his nostrils as she passed. A sweet, beautiful fragrance. Hell, he didn't even like freesias.

Kay joined them, bringing Rochelle and Jackson with her. 'Hey, Lucas, how's your tummy now? All better?'

'It's still sore.' The boy barely lifted his head as he concentrated on the game on his console.

Mario tapped the eight-year-old on the knee. 'What are you playing today?'

Lucas grinned. 'I'm dragon-slaying, and I'm winning.'

'Good for you.' Mario turned to Alexandra and recalled the boy's details for her. 'Lucas presented with sudden severe abdominal pain three days ago. Peritonitis had set in, caused by his ruptured appendix.'

Kay held a thermometer up. 'Open up, Mr Dragon Slayer. Can't have you fighting dragons without making sure you're fit for battle, can we?'

'Mmm-mmm,' Lucas murmured around the thermometer, his fingers never missing a move on the keys.

Alexandra chuckled. 'You're not going to get in the way of his game, Kay.' She leaned around to watch the small screen. 'Hey, watch out, there's a dragon coming out from behind that tree. Yes, that's it.' She clapped her hands. 'Well done. Oops, there's another one.'

Mario gaped. This woman turned into marshmallow whenever she was around kids. As though she knew what kids liked. Did that mean she did have her own family? No one had mentioned one, but then he'd never thought to ask. Why would've he wanted to know? Perhaps he should borrow Lucas's console and play a game during his meeting with her. If he let her slay more dragons she just might begin to thaw with him.

Then Alexandra straightened and stepped across to the next cubicle. 'Hello, Amy. I hear you've been in for over a week this time.'

The twelve-year-old with nephrotic syndrome dropped the book she'd been pretending to read. 'Yeah, it sucks.'

Alexandra picked up the notes from the end of the bed and perused them. 'You've had more infections.'

'The same old thing. I wanted to go home yesterday but Mario said I had to wait a few more days.' She directed a conniving look at him from under her eyelashes.

'Sorry about that. I'm such a mean monster.' He grinned, totally unfazed by Amy's wish to manipulate him.

'But I can go tomorrow, can't I?' Amy asked.

He took the notes from Alexandra and scanned them. 'Keep this up and I can't see why not.'

'Cool. Mum's going to be happy about that. My uncle and aunt are coming to stay and she won't want to be stuck in here with me.' Her tone turned wistful. 'I want to see them too.'

As they finished the ward round Alexandra turned to Kay. 'Dr Forelli and I will be in my office. We're not to be interrupted unless it's an emergency.'

Kay grimaced, glanced at him, then back to Alexandra. 'Of course.' And then she gave their boss a gentle smile. 'Welcome back to the real world.' Kay widened her smile. 'We're glad you're back, by the way.'

'I'm very happy to be back.' Alexandra returned the smile before turning away. That confusion had returned, lacing the glance she flicked him. Did she add 'I think' under her breath?

Alex sank down behind her desk and flicked through that small pile of paperwork she'd noted earlier. At the very bottom was an A4 envelope with 'Mr Mario Forelli, Paediatric Surgeon' typed across the middle. His credentials? She tapped the envelope corner against the desktop. Should she read it now? With Mario watching her?

Sitting opposite her, one long leg crossed over the other, his intent gaze disconcerted her, as if he saw right through all her carefully erected barriers. Yet at the same time he warmed her from the inside out, reminding her body of its sensuality.

Putting the envelope down Alex reached for the piping hot coffee Averill had just brought them. Then, pulling her shoulders back, she asked, 'What happened to John Campbell? He was meant to be here until the end of this week.'

Mario's mouth twisted left, then right. 'He was a no-show. Apparently he got a better offer in Perth where he stopped over on his way out to New Zealand.'

'The rotten so-and-so.' Anger gripped Alex as she recalled that Skype interview and how convincing Campbell had been. 'He sounded so excited to be coming here. Kept on about how New Zealand had been one of his dream destinations for most of his life and to work here would be wonderful.' He'd played her for a fool. 'Do you think he'd arranged an interview in Perth before leaving London?'

'Who would know? But I suspect so. He's never explained his actions to the board.'

Had she wanted the man to cover for her so badly that she'd overlooked something? It had been hectic back in those weeks leading up to her departure. The department had been undergoing renovations, patient numbers were way up. She'd been afraid she'd have to cancel her trip. Then Campbell made enquiries about a short-term position in Nelson. He had excellent credentials. It had been a no-brainer to take him on. 'Guess I didn't read him as well as I'd thought.'

Mario shrugged. 'Fairly hard to do in one interview, especially when it's done from opposite sides of the world.'

'So how did you come on the scene?' As she asked, more questions were popping up in her mind. Personal questions that had nothing to do with him working here. Nor were they any of her business. But for some inexplicable reason her interest was piqued.

Mario's gaze dropped briefly to the envelope on her desk before he answered. 'I walked into the department to speak to the HOD about the possibility of getting a position in the near future. Liz literally grabbed my arm and dragged me up to see the board chairman who all but locked me up until I signed a contract covering your leave.' He gave a wry laugh. 'He was frantic. I could've come with a kindergarten pass and got the job.'

She rolled her eyes. 'Sure. I'm supposed to believe that?'

Mario grinned with all the confidence of a man who knows his worth, then turned serious. 'About Liz.'

'How's she keeping? Her baby bump must be getting quite big now. Nearly seven months along, isn't she?' Lucky girl. A wee flare of envy twisted through her. The older she got, the harder her decision never to have a family was to accept. Her body clock ticking louder than her common sense? But one reminder of what had happened nine years earlier and the clock quietened.

'She's having problems with her pregnancy.'

'Ouch.' Alex winced. Guilt at her brief moment of envy was pushed aside by concern for Liz. 'That's so unfair after all the trouble it took for her to get pregnant.' Liz and her husband had taken more than a year for her to conceive. 'She must be really worried.'

Mario cleared his throat. 'She's beside herself with worry, which isn't helping. Her blood pressure is far too high, especially for twenty-nine weeks. And she's got mild oedema. Three weeks ago she was ordered to take complete bed rest for the remainder of her term.'

Alex felt her jaw drop. 'Is the baby going to be all right? How's Liz dealing with this? Why wasn't I told about this straightaway? It's not as though Kay and others didn't regularly keep in touch with me.'

'It was deliberate that you weren't told. When Liz first started having difficulties she didn't want you told, believing you'd be on the first plane home. Then when she had to stop working I had a talk with Jackson, Mathew and Linley. We agreed we could manage for three weeks. I'm sorry if you feel left out of the loop but we were backed by all the staff. Everyone said you should finish your time away. It might be hard to accept but your staff thinks the world of you and wanted to do the right thing by you, even if you'd have wished to be here.'

The understanding gleaming out at her from those pewter eyes stopped any retort she may have uttered. 'It must've been hard, one person down.'

'We coped,' he said, covering a yawn with one large hand.

'I can imagine how hard that was.' Studying him while trying to grapple with Liz's news she suddenly noticed dark shadows below his eyes, strain lines at the corners of that beautiful mouth. Exhaustion came off him in waves. 'Looks like you've worn yourself out.'

'Ahh, I can't blame Liz for that. I have a four-year-old who doesn't know the meaning of sleeping at night.' Worry clouded his eyes, darkened the pewter to charcoal. 'Too many shadows in the night even for me to vanquish.'

Alex felt her heart squeeze for this unknown little girl. To be afraid of anything was awful, and sad, especially for such a young child. 'Kiddy monsters.'

'Something like that, yes.' Uncrossing his legs he sat up straighter. End of that line of talk.

That was okay. She still had plenty of other questions. 'Where have you been working before turning up on our doorstep? Did you train in New Zealand?'

Around another yawn he told her, 'I did my

medical degree in Christchurch, specialised in London with paediatric surgery being my area of expertise. After that I moved to Florence where I ran the paediatric department in one of their hospitals for four years.'

'Florence?' Mario was Italian? 'That explains the cadence in your voice.' When his eyes widened heat shimmered in her cheeks. She'd just given herself away. Big-time. So what? The guy had a sexy accent. She wouldn't have been the first to notice or comment. It didn't mean she wanted to climb into bed with him. Did it? Shifting in her chair she looked everywhere but at the disturbing Mario, waiting impatiently for the colour to fade from her face.

Thankfully he chose not to pick up on her blunder, instead explaining, 'I'm a born and bred Kiwi, went to the boys' college across the road.' He nodded towards her window. 'My parents grew tomatoes in the Wood, along with other Italian families in the district.'

'So why Italy?' As long as he wanted to talk about himself she was ready to listen.

'My grandparents came out here from Florence when they were first married. All my life I've wanted to know my relatives over there so the job was perfectly placed.'

'You've still got family here?' Italians had large families, didn't they? Lots of siblings, cousins, aunts and uncles, to have fun with, to support one another, to share life's ups and downs. Family. The one thing lacking in her life. The one huge thing. But she didn't deserve family, especially children. No, even her dogs were fictitious, bounding across the pages of the children's books she wrote and illustrated. She focused on Mario, away from her own problems.

That appealing grin was back. 'Sort of. Mamma and Babbo went over to Italy at the beginning of the year and don't look like coming home any time soon. Two of my sisters are married to Italian nationals, and one sister lives here.'

'Is your wife Italian?'

The grin slowly disappeared and he studied his hands with intensity, a frown creasing his brow. 'Sophia's mother was a Kiwi. Unfortunately she died in a diving accident two years ago.'

Gasp. No wonder the little girl had trouble

sleeping at night. She'd be missing her mother. Hard to understand at that age why Mummy wasn't there for her. This also explained the moments of sadness she saw in Mario's face when he didn't think anyone was looking. 'I'm very sorry to hear that. It must be very hard for you bringing up your daughter on your own.' And working long hours, often six and seven days a week.

Suddenly he looked up and clashed gazes with her, a huge 'don't go there' flashing out at her. 'We're getting off track. With Liz on indefinite leave I've been given a permanent position in your department.' His eyes burned into hers, daring her to argue with the situation.

How could she? She might be miffed that the board hadn't waited to talk the situation over with her but she wasn't stupid. With Liz gone the department was down to two full-time paediatricians and one trainee. Highly qualified paediatricians didn't regularly waltz in the door looking for work. 'I'm glad you came along. As you've already learned we put in some long hours as it is without being short of staff.'

Relief poured into those piercing eyes and he

relaxed back in his chair. 'Jackson is shaping up to be a good paediatrician.'

'Yes, he is.'

How did Mario juggle work and a child? She couldn't begin to imagine what that was like for him. Why hadn't he stayed in Italy if that's where his parents were? His sisters too. Families. They never seemed to work out the way anyone expected. Look at hers. A stepfather who resented her for loving her dad; a mother who couldn't care two cents about her. She'd had a lonely, solitary upbringing after Dad died. Sent to boarding school so that Mum and George could swan off all over the world where the inclination took them. When she married and became pregnant she'd really thought that she'd found her own family. Talk about a misconception. Jonty couldn't wait to leave her after everything went horribly wrong. Don't go there. Not now when she was being scrutinised from the other side of her desk. Mario had already proved how good he was at mind-reading.

She reached for the envelope, slid her finger under the flap.

And Mario stood. 'I'll leave you to read that while I go and check up on Tommy again.'

She stared at the closing door. Now what brought about that hurried departure? The CV in her hand? Unfolding the pages she read quickly. Wow, the guy was a megastar of paediatrics. Warmth stole through her. They could make an awesome team if they worked well together.

But this was her domain, the place she felt in control—of herself and of everything around her. Would Mario try to take away her security by insisting on making changes? Only one way to find out—spend as much time on the ward with him. Without smothering him. He didn't need her hanging over his shoulder watching everything he did.

Excitement trickled along her veins. This could turn out to be fun having a colleague as experienced as Mario. They'd be able to bounce ideas off each other, discuss new treatments.

Her smile slowly disappeared. That was fun? It might be the best she'd had in a long time but it wasn't up to scratch in the enjoyment stakes. Real fun would be being held in those strong arms and kissed by that beautiful mouth. Fun would be a walk on the beach out at her cottage in Ruby Bay, hand in hand with Mario, kicking the sand, watching the gulls swooping and soaring, laughing over silly, pointless things.

Yeah, right. She'd better get a full night's sleep tonight. Otherwise sign up for the loony bin. Because something was desperately wrong with her mind, tossing up crazy dreams like holding hands with a man whom until first thing that morning she hadn't known existed.

Mario shivered when icy wind whipped under his jacket and got through to his skin as he crossed the staff car park at the end of the day. June was the pits. Winter was the pits. Though if he had to live through winter Nelson was the best place to be. The forecast for later on in the week hinted at snow. Maybe on Saturday he'd take Sophia and Gina's boys up to Mount Arthur car park so they could build a snowman and throw snowballs.

Sliding in behind the steering wheel of his family wagon Mario slammed the door and leaned his head back on the headrest to stare up at the dark interior. 'What a horrendous day. Thankfully Tommy survived his cardiac arrest, but he's got problems racing towards him, for sure.'

And then there was Miss Alexandra Prendergast. Annoying, intriguing, worrying. Especially worrying. She'd sparked his libido into life big-time. The last complication he needed right now. Not that he'd turn down an evening in bed with a stunning-looking woman—if he had a babysitter on hand. But a quick romp with his boss was not on. Somehow he doubted Alexandra would be into one-night flings. She was deep, thoughtful and not quite into fun. He cracked his knuckles. So suck it up and forget all about getting naked with the woman. Keep everything strictly professional; ignore the wary looks she gave him when she thought he wasn't looking. Forget that you don't have a private life apart from one messed-up daughter. Sophia is your life now, and she's not getting enough of your attention as it is.

The car rocked as another blast of wind slammed against it. Mario looked around the car park, his gaze following a paper cup as it flew through the air to bang into the sports car parked two slots away. Obviously owned by someone who didn't have a brood of kids to run around the place.

Twisting the key in the ignition Mario groaned when the engine raced but didn't start. 'Not again. Not tonight.'

Last week he'd had trouble starting the engine but he'd cleaned the spark plugs and hey, presto, it had gone like a dream since.

He turned the key again, and again. The whining sound of the engine spoke volumes. Slapping the steering wheel he tugged at the catch to release the bonnet and pushed out into the cold. With a torch in one hand he lifted the bonnet and stood studying the wires, the battery and the spark plugs. Everything appeared to be in order. Huh. Like he knew what he was looking for. Topping up the water and oil had been sufficient until now. He pushed and poked everything, shook some wires that meant absolutely nothing to him, went around to try the ignition again. Nothing but that squealing sound.

Definitely time he took the car in for a service. His fingers pushed through his hair. Damn it.

Why did cars break down right when you needed them? He had to get home before the nanny did her usual sulky thing. If only he had a few hours to find another, more obliging girl to take care of Sophia when he was at work.

'Problem?' One word and Alexandra made it sound so sweet. Not to mention irritating.

He spun around, stared down into the dark pits of her eyes. It was probably just as well he couldn't see her expression clearly in the half-light of the street lamps. No doubt she'd be laughing fit to bust. 'My car's packed a sad.'

'Bad timing, right?' When she waved her keys in the air the locks on the sports car popped.

Of course that red racy thing would be Alexandra's. It suited her. Small, compact and sexy. He might be abstaining but his hormones had taken a hit today. They still knew a great package when they saw one. Working with her just got a whole lot more difficult.

'Very bad timing. I need to get home quickly.' Hint, hint. Would she offer him a lift? Though being squeezed into that sardine can with her might prove to be the hardest thing he'd done all day. Even ten minutes rubbing shoulders would only make him crankier than he already was. But he'd do anything for Sophia, right? So he'd accept a lift.

But she shocked him. 'What exactly is the problem?'

What? You think you're a mechanic now? Are you teasing me? 'I turn the key and all I get is a noise. The engine's not firing.'

'But it sounds like it wants to?'

He was gaping at her, his mouth half open. Not his best look, for sure, but what the hell was this woman on? She was a paediatrician, not a grease monkey. 'Yes, it keeps up a steady noise but doesn't even hint at catching.' He reached for the bonnet, began to push it down. If Alexandra wasn't forthcoming with an offer of a ride, then he had to get cracking with finding a taxi. Sophia needed to be in bed within the next half-hour.

'Wait. Don't close that yet.' She placed her handbag inside her to-die-for car and came over to peer under the bonnet of his people-mover. Make that children-mover. Taking a hot date, namely Alexandra, out in it would be a novelty.

For her, at least. Reaching in, she pulled a spark plug and blew on it. 'Looks okay.'

'I cleaned them a few days ago.'

She checked the rest of the plugs anyway. Under his collar his neck grew warm. Didn't she believe him? Then she moved around to the driver's door. 'Can I?'

He could only nod. Was she trying to make him look a bigger idiot than she obviously already thought him? If so, she was succeeding.

She hopped in and planted her foot hard on the accelerator. 'This might be a bit noisy.' Her fingers twisted the key and flicked it on.

A bit noisy? A screaming banshee wouldn't have been heard over this. 'Okay, okay, stop it, will you? You're going to cook the motor and then you'll have to lend me your car.' An image of Sophia strapped into that tiny vehicle brought a reluctant smile to his lips.

Of course Alexandra couldn't hear him. A cloud of black smoke spewed from the vicinity of the muffler, and still she kept the key in the on position and that tiny foot firmly pressed to the pedal. In the half-light from the car's interior her face looked determined, confident. Her mouth moved. Had she just said, 'Come on'?

Then unbelievably his engine started. It ran rough, coughing, soaring, quietening. The woman behind the wheel eased off on the juice, lifting her foot slowly until the motor ran quietly and sweetly.

Mario's jaw dropped—again. 'Well, damn me, if she hasn't fixed it.'

When Alexandra clambered out and stood in front of him looking oh-so-smug he hurriedly swallowed his astonishment and tried for a look that said he was totally used to women fixing his car. 'What was that all about, then?'

'A build-up of carbon, I'd say.'

'Can't trust that carbon, can you?' Time to get out of here, away from this extraordinary woman before *he* blew a gasket.

Surprisingly she burst out laughing. 'Don't worry. I'm not a car nerd. Years ago as a teen-ager in defiance of my stepfather I bought a car without getting it checked over. It turned out to be a bit of a wreck but rather than selling it and proving George right I went to a night school class to learn basic mechanics. I have to admit those lessons have often come in handy.'

He liked it when she laughed. Her eyes lit up and that upright stance softened a little. 'Not with that sports car, I'll bet.'

'You'd be surprised. It's a bit of a prima donna at times.' Her eyes were full of warmth. For a car?

'You and your stepfather had issues?'

The laughter switched off in a flash. 'Among other things.' Stepping past him she headed for her vehicle. 'I'd better get going. My fish and chips will be ready.'

'So you didn't take a cooking class, then?' The words were out before his brain kicked into gear. She'd probably think he was criticising her.

Looking over her shoulder she threw him a small smile. 'Yes, I did actually. Cooking's good when there's someone to share it with, but plain boring when I'm the only one sitting down to the end result.'

So she lived alone. No partner or children. How lonely that must be. And yet his heart lifted at the thought. 'Hey,' he called as she began to close herself inside her can of a car. 'Thanks for sorting me out. I do appreciate it.' *Even if I'd have preferred it to have been Jackson who'd shown me up.* Hell, even Kay would've been okay, but not Alexandra, who seemed to be more than good at absolutely every damned thing. Miss Perfect? Nah, couldn't be. No one got to be liked as much as Alexandra was on the ward if they were that good.

'See you tomorrow.' She waved and turned her key. Of course her damned car started instantly.

CHAPTER FOUR

'Is YOUR CAR starting all right these mornings?' Alex asked Mario a week later as they settled into chairs in her office.

Averill placed mugs of coffee on the desk and closed the door on her way out, taking all the breathable air with her.

From the annoyed expression that briefly flitted across Mario's face Alex figured he wasn't happy with her. Because she'd got his car going? Had that dented his male pride? Then he should learn some basic mechanics.

'*Sì*. Runs like a dream.' He winced. Then his head lifted and his eyes met hers, sending heat darting through her tummy. 'Thanks again. It would've cost a bundle to get the mechanic to come out at that hour.'

Alex grinned at his discomfort. 'Why do men

have to think they've got a monopoly on engines, fishing and driving tractors?'

Those come-to-bed eyes widened, then the room filled with laughter, catching her unawares, curling her toes in a delicious way. 'It's in our genes. We're expected to know how to change a flat tyre, put out the rubbish and paint the roof. And when we don't there's hell to pay. Our egos suffer, our mates rib us mercilessly and women feel let down.'

'We do? Oh, I see. You're not including me in that statement because I know how to do those things.' Her grin faltered. Wasn't she feminine enough? Is that why men inevitably turned away after a short time into a relationship with her?

'You know how to do *all* those things?' Mario was still laughing.

'I hate fishing. They stink, and as for the bait, yuck. And I've never painted a roof.' Did that win her any feminine points? Her insecurities were ramping up today.

'Phew, for a moment there I thought you were superwoman.'

And that would definitely be a turn-off. 'I try not to wear my cape at work.'

'You don't need to. Everyone knows how good you are with the little ones.' His laughter had stopped and a serious expression settled over his face and in his eyes. He held his hands out, palms up, and lifted his shoulders. 'Over the months you've been a hard act to follow at times. "Alex this, Alex that."'

Stunned, she stared back. 'But you've got an awesome reputation yourself. This morning in theatre everyone talked about the fabulous Dr Forelli and his skills.' There'd been a few giggles and queries as to what his skills outside work might be like but no one had any answers. It seemed Mario wasn't rushing round dating all the available females, apparently happy to be charming them into bringing meals for him to take home. When he wasn't at work no one heard a peep from him.

Mario nodded. 'I am good. Paediatrics is a passion which makes it easier to do a great job, to learn everything necessary for my patients.'

Not shy about patting his own back either. But

then why should he be? His CV was awesome. 'Nelson's children are in good hands, then.' And she relaxed further, adding, 'In two pairs of good hands.'

Mario chuckled. 'We'd better get on with the real work. Discussing patients.' He reached down for a file from the top of a stack he'd dropped on the floor by his chair minutes earlier.

'Before we do that I wanted to ask about the six-month gap from when you left Florence and started here. Care to comment?' The gap didn't tie in with Sophia's mother dying two years ago.

The chuckle died. His pewter eyes became frosty steel. 'No.'

'Is there something I should know that might reflect on your work, previous or current?' She hated secrets, especially at work. It didn't do any-one any favours.

'No. It's personal.' He didn't look away. Nor did that steel lighten.

Making a rapid decision Alex let it go and moved on. 'Fair enough. Who's file is top of that pile?' Maybe some time in the future when they knew each other better he might explain. Or

he might not. She doubted he'd be hiding anything important that affected his career, and if
the chairman was happy with his work history,
then so was she.

Mario didn't even blink. 'Tommy Jenkins.
There's no change with that infection. Better than
getting worse, I suppose.'

'He wouldn't survive worse.'

Those solid, mouth-watering shoulders shrugged
eloquently. 'I talked to Tommy's previous specialist in Auckland yesterday. We agreed it's time to
register Tommy's details with the organ donor
centre.'

When had she developed a shoulder fetish?
Since she'd met this guy. That first night, when
trying to go to sleep after an awful first day back,
she'd had a sudden mental picture of Mario above
her, those shoulders bare and so close she could
run her fingers up and over them.

'Alexandra? Hello?'

*Hello yourself. Get back in the picture. You're
at work, discussing—?* Her mind fished around.
What had they been discussing? Tommy Jenkins. That's right. 'All we can do for Tommy in

the meantime is keep a close watch over him and try to lower the risk of further infections.' Which would be hard. The lad needed people around him at the moment, and yet they could be detrimental to his health.

Mario placed the file on her desk and reached for the next one, hopefully unaware of the fantasies spinning through her head. 'Caleb Kernan, tonsillectomy and adenoidectomy. Previous glue ear and repeated throat infections. Taking too long to recover from surgery. I'm running more tests looking for an underlying cause of his lethargy.'

'Why did you change the admission process for our non-urgent patients? It worked the way it was.'

His head jerked up. 'It works even better this way.'

Loud knocking on the door interrupted anything else Mario might've said. A nurse Alex recognised from ED burst into the room. 'Mario, you've got to come. Now. Sophia's in PICU with a silent chest.'

Mario's chair smacked against the wall as the

man moved incredibly fast for someone so big. All the colour drained from his face. His eyes filled with fear. 'How long's she been here?' he demanded as he charged after the nurse.

Nurse Epping, wasn't it? Gina Epping. That's it. How did she fit into the picture? His new wife? Girlfriend? Gina could be an Italian name. So?

Alex automatically chased after Mario. This was an emergency. On her ward. The patient was his daughter, which meant Mario couldn't treat her.

Compassion tightened Alex's chest. Parents found watching their children suffering incredibly difficult. Every parent she'd met, and there were many, would've given their soul to swap places with their desperately ill children.

Her feet tripped over each other.

She'd have swapped places with Jordan. If she'd been given the opportunity.

Her precious baby boy had never had the chance to open his eyes and see the light of day, had never known her love, or turned to her for answers to life's questions. All the things she'd been so excited about sharing with him. Loving her child, giving him everything he needed, sheltering him, guarding him like a lioness, showing him how the world worked. They'd have been a family—her, Jordan and Jonty. Instead she'd been left behind to put the shattered pieces of her life together into a different shape than it had been before. Her heart jerked under her rib cage. It had been many years since she'd laid her son to rest, yet it seemed like yesterday. No, it seemed like today.

Concentrate. This situation was not about her. But it was odd how she'd suddenly started having these moments again. The nightmare, the unrealistic dreams of happy-ever-after scenarios, wondering what it would be like getting up close and naked with Mario.

Maybe the job was taking more out of her than she realised. After one week back? Get real. Another oddball idea waltzed across her brain. What if she did cut back on her hours? But that was plain crazy. The board wouldn't allow it, the ward couldn't manage, and she'd go bonkers trying to fill in the hours.

It's not supposed to be about filling in time, rather about getting a life beyond this place.

Yes, right. Another day, perhaps. In the dim, dark future.

Mario thought his chest would explode with fear. Unbelievable pain ripped him apart. His baby couldn't breathe. 'Does she know I'm coming?' he yelled at Gina. 'Hang in there, Sophia. Daddy's coming. Daddy loves you. Keep breathing. I know it's hard, darling, but do it for me, for you, for us. Keep breathing.'

Gina snatched at his hand. 'She'll be all right, Mario, I promise.'

'Don't make promises like that.' She was tempting fate to intervene and turn the outcome into something too horrible to contemplate. The PICU appeared ahead, the corridor kilometres long. And his baby needed him. 'What happened?' he roared.

'Bridget said she was talking to a friend on her cell phone for a few minutes and when she finished Sophia was gone.'

'A few minutes? More like hours. That phone's attached to her ear. Wait till I see her.'

Gina hadn't finished her explanation. 'Sophia was hiding and when Bridget finally found her she was barely conscious.'

Mario's eyes shut for a brief moment. Hiding again. His little Sophia was still afraid of her own shadow. Anything could send her scuttling into the back of the wardrobe or sneaking out into the garden shed.

Gina was still yapping in his ear. 'It could be time to find a new nanny, Mario. One who loves children more than her phone. Maybe one who'd be happy to live in.'

'The first thing I'm going to do when my little one's safe again.' He kept up his race along the ward. To hell with the rules. They were allowed to run for an emergency and this was definitely an emergency. 'She must've been showing signs of an impending attack most of the morning.'

'She'd been coughing and wheezing, but Bridget thought the wheezing had started getting a lot better.'

'Not better at all.' Sophia's lungs would've been

tightening, thereby reducing the wheezing. A warning sign of worse to come. A warning sign he'd drummed into Bridget's peanut brain a hundred times.

Gina grimaced. 'She's a nanny, not a nurse or a doctor, Mario. Give her a break.'

'I know that but she could try to pay attention.' Was he expecting too much? All he asked was that the girl call him any time she thought Sophia was unwell. A quick text message would've worked. But, on a deep, heavy breath, he acknowledged his guilt. At the end of the day Sophia was his responsibility. His alone.

His shoes skidded, screeched on the floor, as he spun into PICU. Then he was there, standing at the end of the bed, hands on hips, huge gasps filling his lungs with oxygen, staring down at the adorable bundle that was his daughter. Only right now the sight was terrifying. Her eyes were closed, her little chest barely rising and falling. The oxygen mask covering so much of her face isolated her from him.

Mario slipped around the bed to reach for her tiny hand lying on her tummy, curled into a fist.

From the very first moment he'd set eyes on Sophia he'd fallen in love with her. Her big, wary, brown eyes had sucked him in and locked his heart around her. At three years old she hadn't trusted a soul, couldn't rely on any adult to always be there for her. Nearly a year later they hadn't made as much progress rectifying that as he'd have liked. It was going to take him a very long time to prove he would never leave her.

'Jackson, what else have you given Sophia other than oxygen?' Alexandra asked in a calm, no-nonsense voice from the opposite side of the bed.

Mario lurched. Obviously Alexandra had followed him. Now she was focused entirely on his daughter, listening carefully as Jackson told her the dosage of Beta 2 agonist he'd set up for Sophia to inhale. She can't have hesitated when Gina had barged into her office, obviously as quick to respond as he'd been. Mario felt gratitude on top of his fear. Not that Alexandra wouldn't have come, but still. He was glad she was here.

'Did you apply a spacer, Jackson?' Alexandra asked quietly. 'What else have you done?' Her calm voice settled Mario a little. If one of the best paediatricians in the country was on the case, then Sophia was in good hands.

The intern glanced across to Mario, his nervousness apparent as he hesitated, and when he spoke it was to Mario, not Alexandra. 'We've only had her for ten minutes. Gina brought her straight to us from ED.' He drew a breath. 'I haven't done a peak flow yet. Thought it best to start treatment immediately I'd established this was a severe asthma attack.'

'You did the right thing,' Mario murmured, crossing his fingers it was enough. How many times was he going to have to go through this agony? Watching and tearing apart inside as his child did the one thing he could not do for her— fight to live.

Alexandra supported him. 'That's right, Jackson. In severe asthma attacks always treat the patient first, get them breathing.' She took Sophia's wrist, felt for her pulse. 'But the obs need to be done now.'

Mario watched her lips moving as she counted, her eyes fixed on her watch. When she'd finished she ever so carefully replaced Sophia's arm on the bed. Her eyes clashed with his, sympathy flowing towards him. 'One hundred and thirty.'

The knot in his stomach tightened painfully at the abnormal result. An acute attack. His eyes fixed on Alexandra's forefinger running a gentle track down the back of Sophia's hand, as though she was willing his girl to pull through.

Then Alexandra asked, 'Has Sophia had many severe attacks?'

'One's too many,' he snapped. The sympathy in those eyes would undo him as much as the frightening sight of his beautiful girl. If he let it.

Gina's fingers dug into his shoulder as she answered for him. 'Sophia's been having asthma attacks for as long as we've known her, but this is the worst yet.'

Even as Alexandra's eyes widened at this information he was acknowledging this was definitely the worst Sophia had suffered. Damn it, what sort of doctor was he if he couldn't take care of his own daughter, couldn't prevent these terrifying events? What sort of father left his precious child with a nanny all day? A scatter-brained one at that.

He'd thought working at this hospital only minutes up the road from home would be a better option than flying across to Wellington for days at a time. Days when he'd left Sophia with Gina and her boys, and the nanny. As if Gina didn't have her hands full with her three boys and a broken marriage to sort out. He hated that he'd had to rely on her to help him out. Worse had been the days when he hadn't got home to kiss Sophia goodnight, to read her a story, to feed her dinner. Those things had made him question whether he was any better at parenting than Sophia's mother had been. He'd really believed returning to New Zealand had been the best option for them both. But now? Looking down at his reason for living he asked silently, *Do I promise the gods that I'll give up my career if they save Sophia?* He got no answer.

Alexandra continued talking with Jackson, asking about what he'd do next, encouraging him to run through his treatment and the reasons for it, quietly but firmly underlining the necessity of waiting twenty minutes after the initial treatment before giving another dose. As she talked, Mario felt some of his tension ease off. Forget asking the gods to look out for his daughter. He and Sophia had Alexandra Prendergast on their side.

Not to mention Jackson, Kay and Rochelle, all working together to save Sophia.

He went back to watching and waiting, Sophia's tiny hand still tucked into his. She would make it. As a doctor he believed that. As a dad? Twenty minutes was a lifetime to wait to see if the treatment was working. 'Come on, little one. I'm here for you. No one's going to hurt you again. Nor am I going to abandon you. You're mine, a Forelli, and Forellis look out for their own.' Even if he wasn't doing such a good job at it all of the time.

Alexandra asked, 'Is there anyone else you want here with you, Mario?'

'No.' Oh, hell. 'Sorry. I mean, there's only us here. On my side anyway, and Sophia doesn't have any relatives on her mother's side.' This woman was already learning more about him than anyone else had in the past year since he'd first begun his search for Sophia. From the day he'd found out he was a father his sole purpose in life had been to track down his daughter and bring her home. He hadn't wasted any time on small talk, only speaking to those who might be able to help him in his search. Even when he'd finally found Sophia he'd not eased up on his reticence to share what Sophia's mother had done to her. It had been too huge, too unimaginable, not to mention life-changing, to share. And yet slowly, one by one, he was letting out details to Alexandra. They may not add up to much yet, but if he kept on this way she'd one day have a complete picture.

Thankfully Kay changed the subject. 'That reminds me. Mario's got surgery at two.'

Alexandra beat him to a reply. 'I'll need to go over the cases with you, Mario, but otherwise leave everything with me. I'll get Averill to bring the files in here so you won't have to leave Sophia's side. At least until you know she's going to be all right.'

All right? Sophia had years to go before then. First she had to learn what love was, how unconditional it could be. She had to stop getting distressed and run-down so that her asthma didn't keep getting increasingly serious with each new attack. But Alexandra was talking about now, today. She didn't know Sophia's history but she was supporting him—as a father, and as a colleague, which showed she'd gone some way to accepting he worked with her. 'Thank you.' He met her steady gaze, and nodded, repeated, 'Thanks, I appreciate it. I'll be spending the night here.'

Alex watched Mario sitting with his wee daughter, his eyes filled with such love and tenderness, with fear and worry, that her heart swelled. There was no doubt about his devotion. It struck her hard. He'd be just as loving and loyal to the woman he married. Despite what he'd said he seemed to balance family and work well. He would never be remote or too busy for his family.

She glanced at his hands. Big, capable and oh-so-tender when they touched, soothed, Sophia.

Turning to Gina she tried to work out where they fitted into each other's lives. There was little family likeness, Gina being blond and slight. 'So you two are related?'

Gina and Mario looked startled, as though they thought everyone knew that, then both grinned identical grins. 'For our sins, yes.' Gina gently slapped Mario's back. 'My brother was the spoilt one. He had me and our sisters running around after him from the moment we could walk.'

'Yeah, yeah, you were so hard done by. I never had a moment's peace with you lot.'

'Sometimes we'd find Mario reading with a torch in the wardrobe. He used to say it was to get away from us but we knew he was hiding so he didn't have to pick the tomatoes.'

Mario rolled his eyes. 'As if.'

There was something about the easy banter between Mario and his sister that sent a splinter of envy twisting through Alex, further underlining her solitary state. *Oh, get over yourself.* But it wasn't easy, especially when she watched Mario with his daughter and sister. She sighed away the mood and got back onto safe ground the only way she knew how, asking Kay, 'Are Sophia's obs improving?'

'Barely.' Kay handed her the page she'd written results on. 'I'll put Rochelle on to special her.'

'Jackson, I'd like you to continue to keep an eye on Sophia too. If you have any concerns call on Matthew. I'll get Linley to run my diabetic clinic while I take over Mario's surgical list.' As she mentally ran through the doctors and nurses available she studied the little girl's breathing. 'You might want to measure Sophia's peak flow now.'

Alex was reluctant to leave. Mario, despite his sister's presence, looked very alone. Just like other parents she'd observed over the years. No one could quite feel the pain and fear he was feeling right now. That was his alone. She leaned against the end of the bed. 'Mario, is there anything I can get you? Do for you?'

His head came up slowly, as though he couldn't bear to tear his sight away from his little girl as she laboured to breathe, almost as if he was breathing for her. But when Alex could look into his eyes she saw surprise, and gratitude. 'Not at the moment, Alexandra. But I'm glad you offered.'

She held her breath. There was a connection there between them. Something had gone down, yet she didn't know what it was. But it felt right, life-changing even. Then she shook her head. Who was she fooling? She was letting the moment get to her. It wasn't as though she'd at last found a man she might like to get to know well.

Even if she had it wasn't going anywhere. She wasn't meant to be a part of a family, remember? Oh, she remembered all right, but right now she'd happily forget the past tragedies and take another chance. Which went to show how those beautiful grey eyes had hoodwinked her. She would not, could not, be a part of this family. The price was too high, to them and to her.

Her father's death when she was twelve had devastated her, and left her stranded in a lonely life where her mother barely acknowledged her and her stepfather thought no more of her than a pesky fly hovering around him. It had taken numerous knockbacks for her to accept not all fathers were fun to be with. She'd believed she'd fixed her life when she and Jonty married and got pregnant with Jordan. But once again she'd been left behind, bewildered, grief-stricken and alone.

So no matter the sense of longing Mario evoked

in her nothing was going to happen between them. She had to look out for her heart.

Alex leaned back as far as possible in her chair, tipped her head back and closed her eyes. It was after eight o'clock in the evening and she should be heading home. Instead she concentrated on straightening out the kinks in her spine after six hours in theatre by rolling her shoulders left, then right, did the same with her hips. Click, click, went her spine, but the headache behind her eyes continued throbbing. Her back seemed more reluctant than ever to put up with the bending required to perform surgery.

'Hey, there, you look exhausted.'

She snapped forward, sending the headache from a low throb to a pounding. 'Mario. I was about to come over to PICU. How's Sophia doing?'

Without waiting for an invitation he dropped into a chair and put his feet up on her desk, crossing his ankles. 'Sleeping. Breathing normally with a little help. We seem to have got through this attack intact.' He scrubbed his hands down his cheeks. 'Until next time.'

'How do you manage this all on your own?' Why hadn't he stayed in Florence where he'd have help?

Mario put his hands behind his head and stared up at the ceiling. 'There is the nanny, though for how long I'm not sure. And then Gina helps a lot, though she's bringing up three boys on her own since her husband decided he liked single twenty-year-olds without stretch marks on their stomachs. We share Bridget whenever Gina's at work. In the weekends if I'm working Gina tries to fit Sophia in with her lot, and when I'm not here I try to take the boys out. All these kids are why I own that wagon you got going for me. I seem to spend my spare time transporting noisy, boisterous Forellis from one side of town to the other and back.'

'The Italian way.' Certainly not her family's way.

'Isn't it every family's way?' Those steely eyes were scrutinising her. 'Guess I got lucky, huh?'

'You have no idea.'

'Alexandra?' His voice was soft, caressing in its query. 'Are you all right?'

'Of course I am,' she growled. Quickly shaking away the envy she redirected the conversation onto safer ground. 'Who's sitting with Sophia?'

'Jackson offered to hang around while I took a break. I think he's hoping Gina will pop in.' His hand dragged over his light stubble. 'Poor guy. I should warn him he's got a long wait. Gina's still so angry at her ex. But she's mesmerised Jackson.'

'So the charm thing runs in the family.' Mario had certainly got more than a smattering of that gene.

He grinned, a long, slow, heart-melting grin. 'Me a charmer? Where did you get that idea?'

She'd been battling it for days now. Try as she might to keep this sexy, intriguing man at a distance as she wrenched back control of her department, he'd managed to worm his way in under her fiercely protected cover. Not liking to admit that, she detoured the conversation again. 'You were working in Florence when Sophia was born?'

Instantly Mario tensed. 'Yes.'

Did the explanation to those missing months in his CV have anything to do with Sophia? Obviously something terrible had happened if Mario thought his daughter needed to come to New Zealand. Had her mother hurt her? Had he taken Sophia away from her mother before she died?

His gaze drilled into her, the granite shade turned charcoal. His cheek twitched. His chest rose as he drew breath. 'Lucy drowned in a scuba-diving accident up in the Bay of Islands.'

No wonder Sophia had her nighttime demons. 'That's terrible. I'm sorry. You must be devastated.'

He hadn't heard. 'I couldn't take Sophia back to Italy, not to all my family when she'd never met them.' He shook his head. 'It was bewildering enough for a little one.'

'I'd say unimaginable.' Probably equally distressing for Mario too. Though he hadn't looked too rocked when mentioning his partner's death. Had she missed something?

His feet hit the floor with a bang and he stood in one smooth movement. For a big man he was graceful. 'Guess you wouldn't want to share some chicken and mushroom casserole?'

Her eyebrows rose. 'Sounds delicious. You been cooking late at night?'

'No, Kay again. She spoils me. Come on, then.' He reached a hand as though to take hers, hesitated and withdrew, quickly turning for the door.

Alex slipped her jacket on. Heck, he'd changed the subject from Sophia to dinner so effortlessly she'd fallen for it. So he didn't like talking about his past. Fair enough, nor did she. She called after him, 'I'd like to check up on Sophia first.'

'She's my very next stop. She might be okay with Jackson but she's still very frightened. I don't want to leave her for long.'

Yet he'd come to find her. To talk to her. 'You're still sleeping over tonight, then?'

'Of course. Thanks for coming to see Sophia. Jackson has been superb, by the way. He'll make a wonderful paediatrician if he goes ahead and specialises. But—' Mario gave an eloquent roll of his shoulders '—I'm pulling strings and asking for you to look over the notes and see for yourself that my girl's fine. Speaking as a parent, you understand.'

Alex smiled, a full smile that lifted her cheeks and warmed her on the inside. 'Of course I understand.' He was a paediatrician himself and yet he'd asked her to see his precious daughter. She felt warmer and warmer.

And her hormones went from a slow two-step to a racing tango.

CHAPTER FIVE

MARIO WATCHED CAREFULLY as Alexandra checked Sophia thoroughly, looking for a sharp intake of breath or the tightening of her fingers on her pen, signs that would tell him Sophia wasn't getting over the attack. So far all was well. But as he watched her gentleness with his girl, something deep inside him split wide open, letting her in. Immediately he squashed done on the warmth permeating his body.

Forget it, Mario. She might be stunningly attractive, intelligent, caring and whatever else I haven't discovered yet, but I ain't going there. I'm not interested. His gut knotted in disagreement and disappointment. *No, really, I haven't got a spare minute in my life now so how could I fit in a demanding woman? There will be no kisses, no lovemaking, no candlelit dinners, for a very long time to come. Especially not with this woman.* Just working with Alexandra would be more than he could deal with at times. But being focused on Sophia hadn't prevented Alexandra sneaking under his skin like an annoying itch. She was impossible to ignore.

Already she'd dented his resolve to remain un-attached, yet he'd swear she wasn't out to snare him. Completely the opposite. Not once had she made a suggestive move or looked as though she wanted to jump his bones. Which he admitted with regret was unusual. Losing his touch?

He should be grateful but his ego was taking a hit here. Didn't Alexandra think of him in any other way than as a doctor? And maybe as a father?

Sadness pulled at him, turning his heart over. A rare loneliness filled him. He'd always wanted a family of his own, and he now had one. But he'd presumed there'd also be a wife to love and cherish. Children should have two parents as well as siblings to rely on and share things with. Once he'd have given anything for that.

Sì. But that was before Lucy. Lucinda Blake had hurt him, sticking the knife in and turning it. Yet that was nothing compared to what she'd done to her daughter. Bile soured his mouth. At least he'd found Sophia and given her a loving home, away from the welfare system, away from an adoption by strangers. Sophia was his family. That was it in a nutshell. There was no room or energy for anyone else. Stunning human dynamo on heels or not.

He hunkered down beside the bed and reached for his girl's hand. 'Sophia, love, it's Babbo.'

Small brown eyes opened, stared at him as they watered up. 'Daddy, it hurts.'

Leaning over he kissed her forehead. 'I know, sweetheart. But you're getting better every minute.'

Then Alex sat on the other side of the bed and picked up Sophia's wrist. 'Hi, Sophia. I'm Alex. Can I count the beats in your arm?'

Mario struggled not to snatch Alexandra's hand away. For sure Sophia would turn in on herself again. Strangers worried and frightened her. A stranger touching her could send her screaming for a corner to hide in. But wonder of wonders his girl was studying this particular newcomer from under lowered eyelids without getting upset. Slowly she pressed a thumb into her mouth and nodded.

Alex continued, not at all disturbed by the heavy silence from his daughter or him. 'I'm a doctor like your daddy. I'm here to make you better. See?' She held up Sophia's arm. 'My finger's making sure you're all right on the inside.'

The thumb slid out. 'Alex?'

A smile softened Alexandra's face. 'Yes, Sophia?'

'Pretty.' The thumb slid back into her mouth.

Mario stared around, trying not to look at Alexandra. Sophia was wrong. Alexandra was not pretty, she was distractingly beautiful. And right now, when his eyes did finally rest on her, she looked even more ravishing as embarrassment flickered in her eyes, across her face and reddened her cheeks.

He had to get out of here. 'Rochelle, I'm going to the kitchen but I won't be long. Press that button if Sophia suddenly goes downhill.' Then stupidly threw over his shoulder, 'Coming, Alexandra?'

Stepping through the doorway he headed for the kitchenette, not waiting to see if Alexandra followed.

Alexandra did join him, trotting along, her short legs stretching out to keep up with him. 'What's the hurry?'

'The sooner I eat, the sooner I'll be back with Sophia.'

'Want me to organise the meal and call you when it's ready?'

A good idea, but everyone ran around after him and he just wasn't ready to let Alexandra do the same. 'Not at all. You asked if I cooked, now I get to show you.'

Her laughter tinkled between them. 'By heating a precooked casserole?'

'It's all in the way I heat it.'

'Right.'

Mario took her elbow and guided her into the tiny annexe the ward staff used for making hot drinks and heating meals. Under his fingers she shivered, and when he glanced down at her he saw confusion gleaming back at him. Suddenly he wanted to know things about her. 'Where did you grow up?'

'Auckland.' The word was flat. A big stop sign shadowed her eyes. Family problems?

'Sit.' He held a chair out for her at the table, then turned to the stove top. 'Any siblings?'

A sigh oozed across her lips. 'Persistent, aren't you?' Her hesitation dragged his attention from the pot he'd placed on an element to her face. All sorts of emotions scudded across her face, not one of them happy. 'No siblings. Dad died when I was twelve. Mother's a socialite who's very good raising horrendous amounts of money for charities. My stepfather is a stockbroker.' She sat and crossed her arms under her splendid breasts.

Mario's mouth dried as he stared at her. *Bella.* She might be tiny but she had all the necessary curves in the right places. That amazing auburn hair had started falling out of its restraints, shining where the light caught it. He itched to unhook the clip and splay those tresses across her shoulders, to burrow his fingers into the silkiness. When Alexandra wasn't annoying the hell out of him by trying to remind him she was in charge she was shoving him sideways with her physical attributes.

Jeez, Sophia's emergency must've rocked him more than he realised. He was not interested in Alexandra's physical attributes. *Liar.*

'You'll burn the casserole.' She nodded towards the cook top.

Spinning around he snatched up the pot and carefully stirred the contents before returning it to the ring, the gas turned low. What had she been saying about her family? 'That's good what your mother does. There's no shortage of people in need of help from charities.'

'Charity should begin at home.' Her fingers picked at non-existent fluff on her navy skirt.

Facing her again, he leaned against the bench, his hands lightly gripping the bench at each side of his hips. Her voice had been barely more than a whisper but he was sure he'd heard correctly. Why was the woman who liked to remain totally in control telling him this? Any moment now she'd wake up to what she'd said and back-pedal so damned fast she'd pass herself on the way. 'Are you saying you missed out on love and attention as you grew up?' As regret filled those beautiful eyes he knew he was right, and added softly, 'How can that be?' If parents weren't there for you, who was?

'I'm sorry. I don't know what came over me to be blathering on like that.' She was off the chair, heading towards the door. 'You know what? I'm not hungry after all.'

Mario reached the door first. Catching her arm, he turned her around and drew her back to the little table. 'Sit down,' he ordered quietly. 'You don't want to insult Kay by not eating her dinner, do you?'

Alexandra did not sit. She looked everywhere but at him. 'I don't think Kay meant for me to share it in the first place.'

The tension in her muscles under the palm of his hand tightened further. His fingers curled with the need to caress her. How would her skin feel under his fingertips? Taste as his tongue stroked her palm? He dropped her arm. This was off-the-page stuff.

Her chin moved as she swallowed. She glanced across at the pot, her nostrils sniffing the air like a retriever. 'It is hard to walk away from that delicious aroma.'

'Knew you'd see reason.' Hell, he should be yelling at her to go, leave him be. She annoyed him beyond comprehension when he just wanted peace and quiet to think about Sophia's latest asthma attack and what could be done about finding a better nanny.

'But I'm strong. I can resist,' and she was gone.

His jaw dropped as he stared at the empty doorway. God, the woman was definitely irritating. Not to mention downright difficult. Now he'd got the peace he craved. But his stomach soured at the realisation that the last thing he wanted was to eat alone.

At a little after six the next morning Alex popped her head around the door of Sophia's room and gasped at the sight of Mario sprawled full stretch on the bed, taking over most of the space, his daughter's thin arms wound around his chest and her head squashed into his shoulder. Alex felt hot tears prick the backs of her eyelids. This is what a father did. Protected, sheltered, cherished his precious child. A long-buried memory of her dad soothing her when she was feverish with measles rose before her eyes. Another of crying with a stubbed toe and Dad reading to her to calm her. Dad kissing her forehead. Mario seemed to know instinctively what Sophia needed from him. Probably learned it from his own father.

With a man like that at her side even she might manage to become an acceptable mother. Huh? Where'd that come from? There weren't going to be any children in her life. She'd had her chance and blown it. But an intangible something had her dreaming dreams that had long ago been dashed. Dreams of a loving husband, children, a house with a yard, real dogs to play with. Blast Mario. He'd unsettled her more than anything or anyone had since her baby died.

In sleep Mario's mouth had lost that jokey facade that he presented to everyone—except her. To her he always came up looking confident and with a 'don't fool with me, I'm as good as you' expression. Now he appeared vulnerable, sad even. But she suspected if his eyes were to pop open right now he'd instantly show nothing but a benign outlook on the world. It would be laced with his inner strength which came through in everything he did.

Except when he slept. This was an oddly intimate moment. Her feet took her closer to the bed. Slowly, carefully, she reached out. The back of her hand lightly grazed the stubble on his chin. A thrill of yearning and tenderness flooded her. A reminder of what she didn't have in her life. What she wanted.

Snatching her hand back she stepped away, and quietly placed a Harry and Bella book on the bedside cabinet. But still she was unable to tear her eyes away from Mario. Her finger tapped her bottom teeth. He seemed hell-bent on stirring up her days by not totally relinquishing his hold on her department and staff. At the same time he twisted and squeezed her heart so that an alien pull towards him caught her at the most unlikely times. Like in the middle of a patient appraisal. Like when she had to discuss meds with Kay. Like now.

Sprawled out as if he owned all the space, his long legs reached the end of the bed, his powerful thighs pushing into the mattress. Her teeth snapped shut on her fingertip. Those thighs sent heat waves rolling through her, thawing the cold corners of her heart, waking up that muscle-tightening need right at her core that had been dormant for far too long.

Dragging her gaze upwards over the masculine bump at the apex of those thighs to the flat plain of his stomach, the wide chest Sophia clung to. What would it be like to make love with Mario Forelli? Possibly life-changing. Definitely exciting. She imagined those thighs against hers, that chest pressing her breasts.

Oh, get over yourself. Nothing is going to happen with this man. He may be the most alluring male specimen she'd ever met but so what? He was firstly a colleague, secondly a colleague. End of story.

Backing quietly out of the room Alex bumped into someone and whipped around. 'Jenny, so sorry. I didn't want to wake Mario and Sophia.'

The night shift head nurse murmured, 'Sophia kept her dad awake most of the night.'

Heading down the ward Alex asked, 'Any other problems during the night?'

'No emergencies, but some patients didn't settle. Just enough to keep us on our toes and out of our cots,' Jenny replied.

'I'll leave Sophia until she wakes.' If Mario had had a sleepless night he wouldn't thank her later for disturbing either of them. 'I can sit with her while Mario grabs some breakfast.'

'You can tell Sophia one of your stories.'

'I brought in a book for her. Do you think she'll like it?'

Jenny stared at her. 'Every kid I've met loves hearing about Bella and Harry. Why wouldn't Sophia?'

'Why wouldn't Sophia what?' Mario appeared in the doorway to the nurses' office, looking dishevelled and grumpy. Stubble darkened his chin and dark curls fell into his eyes. 'Is there something I haven't been told?'

Alex felt her heart swell. Gone was the swagger, the sharp suit, the charming manner. This was a man who'd had little sleep. He looked good enough to eat. Not to mention very worried.

'Nothing's wrong with Sophia. We were talking about books. I was wondering if Sophia would like a copy of *Harry and Bella Go Fishing*.'

A cute smile lifted his tired mouth. His eyes twinkled wearily back at her. 'Stinky stuff? I didn't think she was ready to learn how to fish, but if you think so, then I guess I should be buying her a rod and reel.'

She chuckled. 'It's a children's storybook.'

'I figured as much. Written by the renowned Lexi Gast, I'll bet.'

'You know about my books?' Tongues had been wagging.

'First thing I heard about you when I started here. Everyone's so proud of what you've achieved with your stories. Apparently being a superb paediatrician doesn't compare. They're a dollar a dozen.'

'Everyone—' she waggled her forefingers in the air '—talks too much.' But she liked that they thought enough of her other career to endorse it so well.

'When do you find time to write and illustrate books?'

'During the weekends when I go out to my beach cottage. Or late at night when I can't sleep.'

'You obviously don't sleep much at all, then, if you've found the time to draw all those amazing illustrations.' Mario grinned. 'Yes, I've seen one of your books when Kay lent it to a little girl with bronchitis.'

This was embarrassing. It was one thing to receive a compliment but quite another to have Mario raving on. 'I left a book by Sophia's bed.'

'Why don't you stop by and read it to her? When you're not busy being a doctor, that is.'

'Hopefully she'll be asleep that late at night.' Why did she get so sharp with him? It wasn't his fault she needed to deny her attraction for him. She tried for a softer tone. 'Though if you want a break for food or a shower I can sit with Sophia. If you're okay with that?'

'I definitely need to freshen up.' He rubbed his stomach, drawing her eyes to that part of his anatomy, making her mouth water. 'And eat something. So Sophia's all yours.' Then his eyes darkened. 'Maybe I should wait. She gets very upset if strangers are there when she wakes up.'

'She seemed okay with me last night. Let's try it. I can page you if you're needed.' Suddenly it seemed imperative that she be able to stay with Sophia, to be there when she woke. Like a test. *Can I get on with children other than as a doctor? Would I've been a good mother to Jordan?* Sophia hadn't turned away from her when she was frightened and stressed to the max, so it was possible she'd accept her presence this morning. And there were the dogs to talk about if things got a bit tense. 'Please.' She nearly reached out and gripped Mario's arm in her need to do this, but at the last moment kept her hand tight at her side.

Mario swallowed hard, nodded slowly. 'I'll go and have a shower first. If I haven't heard a peep from you, then I'll head down to the canteen for breakfast.'

Relief and something akin to happiness surged through Alex, making her almost dizzy. 'We'll be fine. You'll see.' She headed for Sophia's room before he could change his mind but hesitated inside the doorway. 'Oh, my gosh. Isn't she gorgeous?' Alex gazed down at the sleeping tot with her thumb jammed in her mouth and her dark curls falling across her brow.

'She's gorgeous because she's asleep and quiet and not panicking about anything.' Mario's voice was soft but Alex still spun around so fast it made her giddy.

She hadn't heard him following her. Two quick breaths. 'You're supposed to be heading to the showers.' *You're not supposed to have overheard me talking about your girl.*

'On my way.' But he didn't move, kept watching Sophia. A deep, slow sigh spilled across his bottom lip. 'She's going to be all right.'

Convincing himself? 'With you there for her how can she not be?'

'As long as she learns to forget the past. It's a terrible burden for one so little.'

'Want to tell me?' Alex whispered, afraid he might stop talking about this if he thought about where he was, who he was with.

With his hands jammed deep into his trouser pockets he continued watching Sophia as though she was the most precious child in the whole wide world. Which she was to him. 'I didn't know she

existed until a year ago. Can you believe that?'
Pain lined his words.

Shocked, Alex was stuck for words. How cruel
could someone be? But of course she didn't know
all the facts.

'Daddy?' Sophia's eyes flew open. 'Babbo,'
she shrieked.

Instantly Mario was at his daughter's side, pulling her body against him. 'Hey, hey, little one,
Daddy's here.'

Sophia curled into him and stuffed her thumb
back in her mouth. Her big brown eyes stared out
at Alex as Mario's hand rubbed her back.

Alex picked up the chart to read the night's obs.
'I can see you're getting better, Sophia.' Guess
she was wrong to think Sophia would be okay
waking up to find her there.

The girl continued staring at her in that unnerv-
ing manner. Alex felt as though she was floun-
dering. What did she say to a child, this child?
No one had taught her how to behave around
children. She managed fine with them as a doctor but now the right words or actions wouldn't
come when she wanted to be more for this lit-

tle one. She wanted to be a friend because the child had obviously missed out on so much in her short life. So what did she say? Or do? Her mind just would not come up with anything that wasn't trite. Was she more like her mother than she'd thought? Oh, no. Please no. She wanted to be loving, caring and fun, not remote and frigid. Like her dad, not her mother.

Mario kissed the head of curls tucked under his chin. 'She usually comes right fairly quickly, though she'll probably sleep a lot today.'

'We'll keep her in for a while yet. Unless you want to take her home and spend the day with her?' Alex asked.

'No, she's better off here. And I can carry on with my duties. I can't leave another round of surgery for you to deal with. I know you've got an oncology clinic this morning.'

'A small one, thank goodness.' Small meant fewer children with cancer on her turf.

'Dealing with those cases knocks you about a bit, doesn't it?'

A sigh huffed over Alex's bottom lip. 'Sometimes I wonder why I chose such a distressing specialty.'

'Because you want to help. Because you care.' Mario kissed Sophia's cheek. 'Hey, pumpkin, Alexandra's going to sit with you while Daddy's having a wash. Is that okay?'

Big brown eyes impaled Alex, full of caution but also recognition. 'Okay.'

Alex felt as though she'd been bestowed a huge honour. 'I've got a story to read you. Do you like dogs, Sophia?'

The little head didn't move.

Slipping her butt onto the bed Alex picked up the book and, opening on the first page, showed Sophia the drawing of two black schnauzers carrying fishing rods and a basket of bones. 'That's Harry.' She pointed to the slightly bigger dog.

'Harry,' Sophia repeated. 'Who's that?'

'Bella. She's carrying lunch. Leftover bones from the family's dinner.'

'I like chop bones.'

'Me too.' Alex settled closer and, bending her head nearer Sophia, began to read.

I could get to enjoy this. The book shook in her hands, her voice wobbled. *I could? Darned right, I could.*

* * *

Mario's feet were glued to the floor. He knew he should be grabbing the opportunity to shower and put on clean clothes, but he was riveted by the sight of Sophia snuggling up to Alexandra.

Sophia didn't do snuggling very often and certainly not with just anyone. Especially not with aloof dynamos. She had to have known them for a while first.

Bet Alexandra didn't nestle into a bed with a young child too often either. Who did she snuggle into bed with? Something akin to jealousy unfurled deep inside. What? He didn't like the idea of Alexandra in bed with another man? Since when? With her tiny frame and worry-filled eyes she did bring out the protective instinct within him but that had nothing to do with not wanting to imagine her with someone else.

Something was going on. Hell, he'd nearly told her about Lucy and the horrendous pain she'd caused, and that said something about his state of mind. Because—his shoulders rose and fell— because he didn't tell anyone what had happened. Apart from his family. He'd hardly have got away with turning up with a very young daughter and no explanation. It had been a year since he'd informed Mamma and Babbo that they had a granddaughter, and that little Sophia was going to need all the love they could give her plus some. The first months Sophia had been in his care had been excruciating. In the numerous phone calls back and forth between Nelson and Florence none of them talked about Lucy and why she'd done what she did. Especially not him, shutting anyone down who tried to raise the subject.

Yet now he blathered on to Alexandra about it. He'd barely started the sorry story but that was loads more than he'd ever let out before. His gaze stuck on her. Again he wanted to finger that hair. It shouldn't be pulled back off her face. Lying free over her shoulders would be much more de-lectable. But that wouldn't become the position of HOD. This woman tried hard to keep her distance from her staff, to make them remember every moment of the day she was in charge. And thankfully failed. Everyone knew their boss was marshmallow.

Mario wished the sweet smile she gave Sophia

could be directed at him. Just then she raised one hand and scooped Sophia's curls back off her forehead and Sophia turned her cute little face and thanked Alexandra with her own sunny smile.

Mario's stomach crunched. Wow. For the first time since he'd known his daughter he'd seen her turn to another person who wasn't family, a person she'd only met the night before under frightening circumstances. Warmth slid through him, relaxed that part of him that constantly worried about Sophia. Who'd have believed it would be Alexandra who'd get through to his daughter? Two lost souls recognising something in each other?

What he didn't get was why Alexandra should be so lost. Everything she did seemed to turn to success.

'I don't believe it,' Gina whispered over his shoulder.

Raising his finger to his lips, Mario tipped his head in the direction of the nurses' station. 'Come on,' he whispered. 'We'll leave them to Harry and Bella.'

'Alex's reading her the dog story? But Sophia's afraid of dogs. Even seeing them on TV sends her screaming to you.' Gina sounded as perplexed as he felt.

'Apparently paper dogs are okay.' Did everyone know about Alexandra's books? Then the tantalising smell of warm cheese distracted him. 'Is that my breakfast?' He pointed to the bundle she carried in one hand.

Gina handed him the cloth-wrapped parcel. 'Straight from the oven. The boys wanted chocolate muffins for their lunch boxes so I threw in a batch of cheese ones for you.'

'Did I tell you you're the best sister?' Gina might have a load of her own problems but she still came through for him all the time. It might be selfish of him but he was grateful she hadn't followed the rest of the family to Italy.

'How many times have I heard you say that to any one of us?' Gina grinned at him.

A vision of Alexandra, her eyes brimming with longing for a close-knit family, snapped on in his head. She really didn't know what it was like to have people there for her. Even if she hadn't said as much it had been blatantly obvious in those sad eyes. He used to take his family for granted, but not since Sophia's arrival. With her fears about being left again stabbing at his heart he'd quickly realised how lucky he and his sisters were. Not once in their lives had they even thought they weren't special to their parents or their siblings.

'Hey.' He slung an arm around Gina and hauled her in against him. 'Thanks. For everything.'

Squeezing him back she pulled free. 'No problemo.'

See? Gina knew exactly what he'd been on about without any explanation needed. They were close, understood each other at a glance. That was family. That was the most important thing in life. Maybe Alexandra didn't have that. Nor would she be getting it from him or his.

Then Gina blew him apart. 'You should try to get to know Alex better, bring her close. She'd be perfect for you.'

Shock exploded through Mario at this traitorous statement from his sister. She should know better. She did know better. 'No,' he bellowed. 'No way.'

Gina smiled that infuriating know-it-all sister smile at him. 'Shh, you're disturbing the ward.'

'Stuff the ward. Where did you get that half-baked idea? Huh?'

'By watching you whenever Alex is within touching distance. You only have to hear her voice and you're on alert. And look at you. You never shout, especially at work, but what have you just done?'

'I am not shouting,' he shouted.

Kay popped her head out of her office. 'Everything all right here?'

Mario glared at Gina, then at Kay. 'Why wouldn't it be?'

He spun around and strode past both meddling women, intent on having breakfast, but as he passed, Kay quipped cheerfully, 'Gina's right. Alex is behaving the same way.'

Bollocks. Nothing, no one, in this world could distract that fierce woman from whatever held her attention at any given time. His shoes screeched when he whipped around to stare Kay down, put her in her place. 'I'm sure you have more important duties than delving into my personal life.'

Kay didn't even blanch. No, damn it, she winked, first at him, then at Gina, who laughed.

'You are so screwed, brother.'

'You— You—' He spluttered to a stop, threw his hands in the air. An image of Alexandra slapped against his mind. Alexandra walking with her head high and her back ramrod-straight, that mass of hair he had yet to see spilling free down her back plaited tight into her head, yet another whiter than white blouse a stark contrast to yet another navy suit. Deep inside him something further gave way, letting warmth into places that had been iced over since Lucy did the dirty to him. No!

Jerking his head around, his eyes clashed with his sister's knowing look. 'You're wrong,' he told her. *You have to be.*

He'd met Alexandra far too late to give her what she needed. He didn't have spare hours to wine and dine her. Sophia wasn't ready for siblings. His heart thumped once. In disappointment? Nah, couldn't be. He wasn't interested.

Trying to convince yourself? Trying too hard to prove Alexandra hasn't got under your skin? Into your psyche?

Mario turned away, closed his eyes, concentrated on bringing up a picture of Sophia and only saw a small, auburn-haired firecracker of a woman standing glaring at him, daring him to step outside his comfort zone.

Hell. No way. He stormed down toward the staff bathroom, trying to outrun his mind, outrun that delectable, annoying image. Except already he was getting used to her, getting used to the fact that she didn't roll over to have her tummy scratched like every other female he came in contact with.

His steps slowed. Alexandra was being wonderful with his daughter, giving selflessly as she did with everyone. More importantly, Sophia hadn't spurned Alex. He'd never have believed that if he hadn't just seen the way they were cuddled up together. Perhaps Sophia was a better judge of character than her father. Maybe he'd got it all wrong. It wouldn't be the first time.

Lucy had told him she loved him, promised to

marry him, then disappeared out of his life one night, never to return. The only thing she'd left behind was a note to say she'd couldn't live with him any more, that he never had enough time for her and that his family completely overwhelmed her.

She hadn't told him she was pregnant with his baby.

She didn't tell him she'd given Sophia up to the welfare system.

She'd been proof of how bad he was at reading women.

CHAPTER SIX

'HEY, AMELIA, HOW'S that maths homework going? Solve those pesky problems?' Mario asked as he lifted the girl's notes from the end of her bed.

The redhead wrinkled her nose in disgust at him as only ten-year-olds could. 'It's too easy. I bet I get one hundred per cent.'

'Are you any good at chess?' Mario grinned at Amelia, while sadness gripped him for this kid who knew nothing about playing on the back lawn with a bat and ball. Seemed her parents were driven to make her a scholar, obviously missing the point that there was more to life than classrooms and lessons. Even their trip to Fiji had been to learn about the local flora and fauna, not to lie on the beach or swim with the fishes for fun. Unfortunately Amelia had found out the hard way about mosquitoes and the diseases they carried.

'The best. I beat Dr Linley yesterday.'

For a ten-year-old that seemed the wrong answer to Mario. But, 'You should ask Jackson to play against you. He's good.'

'I will.' Amelia stretched upright against her pillow. 'My temperature's still too high, but I got through the night without any convulsions, so I must be improving. Another blood test to check my CBC today?'

Mario grinned at this precocious child. 'You should be almost better by now. And yes, I'll arrange for the lab to take a sample this morning.' Replacing the notes he stepped around the bed. 'But first I have to check your lymph nodes.'

'They've gone down a lot since yesterday,' his patient informed him.

Feeling under her chin and then around her armpits, Mario had to agree. 'Okay, missy, any nausea after breakfast?'

She shook her head at him. 'No, only disgust at what they gave me.'

Alexandra stepped over from the next bed, shaking her head in amusement. 'Seriously, Amelia, if you're going to be a doctor you'll have to get used to hospital food.' She lifted gut-twisting eyes to him. 'Are you still giving her acetaminophen?'

'Fluids and drugs for today at least. Then if the CBC has returned to near normal I'll dispense with both and think about sending Amelia home.'

'Do I have to go?' Rank disappointment contorted Amelia's face. 'My parents will make me go back to school straightaway.'

'I thought you liked school,' Mario said.

'Not really.' Her mouth screwed up. 'It's kind of lonely. I wish I could do correspondence school.'

And that wouldn't be lonely? 'How about I give you a note to stay at home until after the school holidays. No point going back for one week.' Mario wanted to cut this girl some slack, to make her life a little easier. But in reality there was little or nothing he could do for her once she left his care, which, he reminded himself, was only medical.

Amelia nodded. 'That would work. Thank you, Mario.'

'Jeez,' Alexandra whispered as they turned away. 'I bet she's the school nerd.'

'Yep, and all because her parents have an agenda that doesn't include being a normal kid,' Mario replied quietly as they moved toward the next patient.

'I hate it when parents push their needs onto their children. It's so unfair. What if Amelia wants to be a carpenter?' Her words were underlined with knowledge.

'Is that what you wanted to be?' Mario smiled at the thought of this tiny woman wielding a hammer, and knew she was perfectly capable of it, or anything she set her mind to.

'No, a cabaret singer. My father and I used to push the furniture back against the walls and dance up and down the lounge, singing at the top of our lungs. Mother hated the racket and was forever telling Dad off for encouraging me. She thought I should be studying hard to keep ahead of the crowd. Dad ignored her most of the time, though I did sometimes overhear fierce arguments about it late at night when they thought I was asleep.'

'So you can sing too?' He didn't keep the astonishment out of his voice.

She grinned, a happy, totally unfazed grin. 'I'm tone deaf.'

He laughed with relief. She wasn't perfect after all. 'There ended your cabaret aspirations.'

'No way. It was huge fun.'

'What about the dancing? Do a good Moulin Rouge dancer impersonation by any chance?'

She blinked endearingly at him. 'With legs shorter than a chicken's? I don't think so.'

His gaze dropped to those shapely pins. Nothing chicken-like about them. His mouth dried as he imagined them wrapped around his waist. What was going on here? When he raised his eyes to her face she was grinning, oblivious to his thoughts.

'But I do squawk in the shower sometimes, just for the hell of it.'

'Remind me not to visit when you're in the shower, then.' The words spewed off his tongue with no help from his brain. If he didn't know better he'd have said he was flirting with her, but he wasn't. He couldn't be. No way.

She tripped over her tiny feet as her head flipped further back and her focus clashed with his. 'I can't imagine why you'd be visiting me at all. Let alone me being in the shower at the time.' The words trailed off as her face turned scarlet and her tongue slipped across her bottom lip.

Catching her arm to steady her, Mario's fingertips burned as though touching a hotplate. She *was* a hotplate. A darned hot lady in a tiny, and hot, package. Jerking away he stepped sideways, putting space, air, something, between them.

She stared at him from enormous eyes. 'Oh. Right. Sorry, slip of the tongue.'

Could her brain be as fried as his? Miss Cool turned Miss Hot? He'd swear she wasn't playing games, doubted she knew how to. But she'd managed to fire up the dormant hormones from every corner of his body. Including south of his belt. Especially south of his belt.

He wanted her. Badly.

He couldn't have her. Not now, not ever.

Tell that to his body.

Shut down or take a cold shower.

The threat didn't work.

Mario spun around, charged into the next room and snatched up Gemma Lewis's file to stare blindly at the words and figures dancing before him. Figures. As in numbers, not in a small, compact feminine frame on heels that brought the top of her head to little past his chest. Chest. Breasts. Those sumptuous curves that filled out the front of her blouse drove him crazy with desire whenever he looked at them. Which was why he didn't look. Yeah? Okay, not often.

'Hey, Mario, I'm glad you dropped by while I'm here. I've got some questions for you about Gemma's bowel problems.'

What? Who? His neck cracked as he jerked his head up. Ahh. Judge Lewis. 'Brandon. No court session this morning?' *Concentrate, boyo, or you're in deep doodoos. This is one man you can't fool with medical burble while you're getting everything else back under control.*

'Ten-thirty is my first showdown. Court staff are holding a meeting at the moment regarding pay rates so I grabbed the opportunity to see Gemma.' Brandon stood and shrugged his expensive suit jacket into a more comfortable position. The guy would look more at ease in gumboots and jeans, but Mario wasn't fooled. Brandon had a reputation for being tough on offenders and no one liked coming up on trial in his court. He also spent every spare moment he had here with his daughter, reading stories, playing games. An all-round good guy.

'Fire away with your concerns about Gemma.'

As Mario delved into a conversation about Gemma's continual health issues the heat slowly dissipated from his muscles. The gripping sexual tension eased off enough to stop distracting him. When he'd finished answering Brandon's numerous questions he headed for the coffee maker and a moment's solitude.

Away from the temptation of Alexandra Prendergast. Despite all his rehashing of his previous relationship with Lucy his body—and his brain—refused to ignore Alexandra.

Infuriating. Sexy. Beguiling.

Alex curled up on the couch, her hands clamped around a steaming mug of strawberry tea. Wind-driven rain pelted the windows. Down below streetlights looked all skewed through the torrential downpour which was also putting her off going out to get something for dinner. It would have to be eggs on toast—if there were any eggs in the fridge. Who knew? She hadn't made it to the supermarket all week.

Sipping the fruity tea she wondered where the days had gone. They'd flashed past in a flurry of patients, emergencies, staffing problems and the new specialist. Not to mention his little girl. It seemed only yesterday that she'd returned to the hospital, and been hit with the presence of Mario Forelli.

The buzz of her intercom was loud in the quiet apartment. Puzzled she went to answer it. 'Hello.'

And got the shock of her life. 'Alexandra, it's Mario. Can I come up?'

Blink. Mario? Here? Why? 'Sure.' At least she wasn't singing in the shower. She pressed the button to let him into the building. Her watch showed nine-thirty. Late to be calling on someone, especially someone he didn't know outside of work. Did he want to clear the air over that ridiculous moment on the ward? She'd prefer he didn't bother. Less said the better.

Her heart sank. Maybe there was a different,

worse explanation. Something might have happened to Sophia. Another attack? But she'd been
fine two hours ago when Alex had left. Mario
had intended taking her home when he finished
up for the day. Anyway, he wouldn't be here if
Sophia had become seriously ill again.

Her doorbell rang at the exact moment Alex
looked down at her trackpants and sloppy sweatshirt. 'Oh, heck. He can't see me looking like
this. He'll be laughing for weeks.'

Buzz, buzz. 'Alexandra?'

'Why can't he call me Alex?' Admittedly, when
Mario said 'Alexandra' it rolled off his tongue
like melted chocolate to make her think of sweet
treats and hot kisses. Which was bad, bad, bad.
She certainly wasn't about to be anything sweet
for Mr Forelli, despite the image of a shower and
them both naked under the steaming jets of water.
He certainly wouldn't want to spend any more
time with her than he had to so to heck with her
appearance.

But when she opened the door and Mario
stepped past her without blinking she decided

she could've been decked out in a Madonna bra and he wouldn't have noticed.

Odd how exasperating that was.

Then he handed her a bottle of cabernet merlot. 'Thank you for spending so much time with Sophia in hospital, and for the book you gave her. She's smitten with Harry and Bella. They now sleep under her pillow.' He held out a plastic container in his other hand. 'Another casserole. This time from Averill.'

'Th-thanks. I think.' Alex took the wine and the container from his outstretched hands.

Without being asked Mario slipped out of his coat and hung it on the coat rack, removing a packet of rice from a pocket. 'I thought we could share the food. Have you eaten?'

'Not yet. I was trying to decide what to order from my favourite restaurant over the road. Hard to dredge up enthusiasm when I'd have to go out in that weather to get it. Anyway, it seems too late to bother now.'

He shook his head like a cat shakes its paws after walking through a puddle and droplets of water flew through the air. 'The casserole will fill the gaps. Right, so where you keep your glasses?'

Make yourself at home, why don't you? Alex headed for her designer kitchen that was mostly used to boil water for tea or coffee.

'Sorry, am I being too forward?' Mario was so close behind her he must be almost stepping on her heels. She could sense him, smell his after-shave, feel his breath as he talked. And he read minds. Hers, at least. 'If you want me to disappear, then you've only got to say so. But—'

When he didn't finish the sentence she turned to face him and leaned against the bench for strength as he grinned a slow-burn kind of grin. The sort of grin that had probably got him any-thing and everything he'd wanted throughout his life. Continuing in a low drawl that reached in-side her to tease and twist her nerve endings and spin her blood along her veins at a breakneck speed, he told her, 'But I really don't want to go out in that rain again just yet. Not until I've had a taste of that wine.'

'Here I was thinking you'd brought it for me.' When his mouth curved further upward she moved her head from side to side, trying to negate the sudden warmth swamping her. When that didn't work she abruptly changed the conversation to something less provocative. 'What was so important to tell me that brought you out in the rain?' Stepping sideways she endeavoured to put some space between them, backing across the kitchen.

He stepped into the space. 'I really did want to thank you for being so good with Sophia. You have no idea how wonderful it was to see her relax with someone who was a virtual stranger only a couple of days ago.'

Back two more steps. 'You could've told me all that at work any time of the day.'

He filled the space again. 'Too little effort. You might've thought me a bit offhand.'

'Never.' The next backward step brought her up against the centre counter. Watching Mario as he studied her in return her mouth dried. Deep inside her muscles rolled like an ocean swell. This man was something else. And he knew it. But for once that didn't bother her. He was open and honest. What she saw she suspected would be what she got.

Huh? Like she was going there? This man was a colleague, not a hot date. He'd come to thank her for a small kindness, not to strip her clothes off in a passionate frenzy. He'd brought wine and casserole, not champagne and lobster.

'Alexandra.' He towered above her, his chin almost touching his chest as he looked down at her.

Whipping sideways, she managed to avoid touching him anywhere on that mouth-watering body. 'Why don't you call me Alex like everyone else?' *And don't you dare say you're not like everyone else.*

'You have a pretty name. Why not use it?'

'Only my family uses my full name.' And then it never sounds pretty—or hot.

'Is that why you don't like me doing it?' Could he see right into her head with those eyes that at the moment were the colour of polished pewter, eyes that saw everything, and made her knees knock in a very unladylike manner? Did he know the turmoil going on inside her usually calm body? He probably did. He'd be experienced with women, would be able to read their every nuance. Whereas her? When it came to reading men she was still at kindergarten.

Then he added, 'Alex isn't as feminine as Alexandra.' Slowly his gaze slid off her and he peered around the kitchen. 'You could cook up a storm in here. I'm drooling just thinking about it.'

Feminine. Drooling. The bottle she'd forgotten she held clanked on the marble centre bench. In her other hand the container of food suddenly felt very heavy. For the first time she noticed how wide Mario's mouth was, how full his lips. Bet his kisses were magic.

Bang. The heavy container slid from her lifeless fingers, slammed onto the bench, slid towards the edge. They both reached for it at the same instant. Their hands met, grabbed and saved the meal. Alex tugged free immediately, shaking away the heat that had just poured through her fingers, up her arm, turning her neck red, her insides liquid.

Mario hurriedly stepped away, his chest rising and falling rapidly. When she dared look at him he had thrust his hands deep in his trouser pockets and turned to stare out the window into the black night.

Her tongue licked her lips while her brain tried to get past that stupid mistake of dropping the container, then trying to snatch it up again. A mistake that shouldn't mean anything, shouldn't have her heart thumping like a dog's wagging tail on the floor, shouldn't have her suddenly wishing Mario had come to visit her as a woman he might like to get to know and not as a colleague he had to thank for going that little bit extra with his daughter.

Suddenly she needed wine, not strawberry tea. The cupboard door thwacked back as she reached for two red wine glasses.

'Here, let me.' Mario saved the glasses from her trembling fingers and placed them on the bench.

He seemed so calm, so unperturbed by that touch. But of course he would be. Experienced, remember? She must've imagined his quick breaths a moment ago, while *her* body hadn't returned to its normal half-dead slumber. Her heart rate hadn't quietened down to its usual pace, nor had her knees suddenly found their supportive strength. *Guess if you haven't been running at all and then you try a marathon this is how your body would react—completely out of sorts with itself.* And face it, she hadn't been running, or kissing, for a very long time.

The crack and twist of the bottle top sounded loud between them. The heady scent of a full-bodied red wafted through the air as he poured the nectar into the glasses. And her body remained out of sorts with itself.

Handing her a glass Mario raised his. *'Salute.'*

'Cheers,' and moistening her parched mouth, she savoured the flavour of sun-kissed vines and dark grapes on her tongue. It still didn't fix what ailed her body. Only an hour in her bed with Mario would do that.

Heading for the lounge she sank onto the couch, while Mario followed and crossed to the big windows. Peering out and down, he noted, 'Not much of a view tonight. I wonder how much snow is being dumped up on Mount Arthur right now.'

'Enough to make the hills look pretty tomorrow when the sun pushes through. I can never get enough of gazing at the snow-clad mountains and hills. My first winter here was a novelty. Still is.' Verbal diarrhoea now? 'I wasn't so keen on the frosty mornings when the washing froze solid on the line. Don't do a lot of hanging washing these days, living in an apartment.' Definitely driveling!

'Ever been up the mountain to play in the snow?' Mario crossed to sit on the other end of the couch.

'No, I've never ventured up there.' Not a place to go alone. Who would she throw snowballs at?

'If Sophia hadn't taken sick I'd planned on taking her and her cousins up there for some snow fights this weekend.'

'Sounds like fun.' The wistful thread in her tone embarrassed her but before she could redress it Mario was talking again.

'Heaps of fun. The kids have a fabulous time.'

She loved how when he talked of something he enjoyed his eyes widened and the pewter colour gleamed out at the world. His generous mouth twitched and she had to restrain from reaching to run a finger over his lips. Gulp. Had she reverted to a teenager sometime over this past week? Or had it happened en route from the States, this strange change in her? Since when did she want to touch a man she worked with? Not just touch him, but caress him intimately, to get up close and very personal.

When Alexandra remembered to relax as she talked her face lit up, her eyes shone and her soft mouth curved into a delicious smile lifting her cheeks. She was lovely when she forgot to be serious, when she didn't recall that a lot of tiny Nelsonians relied on her to make them better. *She's lovely all the time. Even in a snitch, when her eyes screw up tight and her mouth flatlines.*

She was telling him, 'I dropped in to see Liz after work, hoping to catch up, but she wasn't home. I hope everything's all right.'

'She and Kevin probably went out for a meal.'

'Guess you're right. Making the most of the time they've got left before junior makes his or her appearance.' Again that wistful tone coloured her voice.

So Miss Prendergast would like kids of her own? Why wouldn't she? Any woman who was as good as she was with her young patients must yearn to be a parent herself. A fleeting image of a string of gorgeous little Alexandras stopped his hand holding the glass inches from his mouth. His tongue stuck to the roof of his mouth. Oh, hell.

She was taking a sip of wine, rolling the liquid across her tongue, savouring the ripe, rich flavour. 'This is good. Thank you, though it wasn't necessary.'

She unfolded her legs from under her butt and stood, stretching onto her toes. Doing more damage to his overenthused hormones. Pink trackpants and sweatshirt. Who'd have believed it? Miss Power-dresser with her array of fitted suits and crisp white blouses did ultra-casual and shapeless?

Forget shapeless. Definitely not shapeless. What the clothes didn't have her curvy body more than made up for. Her pert breasts shaped the front of her sweatshirt perfectly, pushing out the fabric in an enticing manner that had him longing to touch them. Her thighs were taut under the clinging fabric of her pants, sending his blood southward. Again.

This was so not a good look. He needed to go, get away from her before he did something dumb like make a pass at her. How would that go down? Actually, he knew the answer to that. He might as well hand her the axe to take his head off right now. Imagine turning up on the ward on Monday if he'd made a move on her. Frosty would feel warm compared to how she'd treat him then.

Why had he come? It had to be one of the dumbest things he'd done in a very long time.

No, it wasn't. He'd come because she was the first person who wasn't family to get through to Sophia so he'd wanted to thank her personally in a personal setting. Not on the ward, surrounded by sick children and busy nurses and doctors. A film played across his mind. Sophia gripping *Harry and Bella Go Fishing* in her tiny fist, refusing to let go of the book even in sleep. Sophia refusing to lie down until he'd read that story twice more. This was why he'd come to the lion's den. And now he realised he'd made a mistake. He should've stayed away.

'I guess at this late hour you're past wanting to eat?' She sounded hesitant.

Hello? He was thinking sex and she was talking food? A laugh tore through him. Miss Prendergast was so grounding. She might even be good for him. 'I'm never past eating.'

Maybe he hadn't made a mistake. Maybe this was the way to finally knock away those last few barriers Alexandra kept firmly in place between them. He stood and headed for the kitchen. 'Which is the pot drawer?'

Alex rubbed her very full tummy. 'What a delicious dinner. In the past week I've discovered I work with at least two very good cooks.' They'd eaten all the beef casserole, right down to the last delicious scrape of sauce, and every grain of rice Mario had steamed.

The wine had long gone, and now they were back sitting side by side on her couch, their shoulders almost but not quite touching. Empty coffee cups sat on the low table in front of them. The rain had stopped beating at her window, letting the lights below shine through.

'I'm glad you didn't chuck me out when I took over your kitchen.' Mario's hand rubbed lightly down his thigh, drawing her eyes to follow the movement. Right down from the top of his leg to his knee.

'You're more than welcome to it. I hardly get the bench dirty.'

'And thank you for an adult evening. Talk that's got nothing to do with learning to tie shoelaces, a drink that's about enjoyment and a dining companion who's not picking through everything on her plate looking for hidden nasties.'

'Sophia's not a good eater?'

'We're getting there. When I first brought her home I could count on one hand what food she liked, none of it healthy.' His fingers began to play a slow beat on his knee.

Alex stirred, straightening away from his warmth and biting down on the urge to cover those fingers with hers, to lift his hand and place soft butterfly kisses on his palm. His hand was large, would easily cup her cheek and chin. If he did that would he rub his thumb across her hungry lips? Swallow. There'd be no stopping her taking his thumb into her mouth if he did.

'Alexandra.' His voice was almost a whisper, caressing and seductive.

If you touch me, caress me with your fingers as your voice is already doing, then there'll be no such thing as quiet. I'll combust, noisily.

'Look at me, Alexandra.' Her name rolled off his tongue, sending shivers of need through her body, goosing her skin.

Twisting around on her bottom she slowly looked up into his strong face and met his opaque gaze, saw desire flickering back at her. Her own need expanded, reached every place in her body, became sweet heat at her centre. She began leaning forward, closer to the source of this desire, closer to the body that had held her fascinated since she'd first set eyes on him. Nearer and nearer to the man who'd woken her up from a long drought of feeling anything close to desire. These sensations rippling through her body were like flames following an oxygen source. 'Mario,' she murmured through parched lips.

She spread her hands on that marvellous, expansive chest filling her vision. Felt the hard muscle underneath his shirt, knew the moment he quivered. Tipped her head back. All the better to see him. He was unbelievably beautiful.

His hands slipped up her arms, and he caught her elbows to draw her even nearer so that her breasts brushed against him. She tugged her hands from between them, placed them on his waist. Felt his pager begin to vibrate.

Simultaneously her cell phone rang.

They sprang apart like guilty teens, Mario muttering, 'Great timing.'

'Something must be going down on our ward. Hello?' Alex jammed the phone against her ear and turned away to hide the deep blush staining her cheeks. If the phone had rung moments later they mightn't have had the strength to stop and answer it.

Whoa. She should be grateful. She had so very nearly kissed Mario Forelli. And that surely would've been the biggest mistake of her career. No, not quite, but right up there.

'Alex, it's Jenny. You're needed in PICU. Liz is having her baby.'

'Emergency in PICU,' Mario read from his pager simultaneously.

Alex's head whirled. 'But she's not due for weeks, months.' No wonder Liz hadn't been at home. 'We're on our way,' she told Jenny, her skin lifting in chilly bumps.

Alex snapped her phone shut. 'Liz is in labour.' Rushing to her bedroom she grabbed a warm jacket and track shoes, then returned to the lounge to find Mario had switched off lights and was checking the gas was off. 'I'll meet you there. Poor Liz must be beside herself with worry. This is awful.'

'Come with me. I'll drop you home later.' His eyes were full of concern and something else she didn't understand.

Alex slipped her hand into the crook of his arm. 'Let's go.'

CHAPTER SEVEN

'LIZ, GO TAKE a shower and grab some sleep.' Alex draped an arm around her friend's waist. 'I'll stay here with Chloe until you get back. That's a promise.'

'She's so little. How can she possibly survive?' Liz remained still, her voice wooden as she stared down at her fifteen-hour-old daughter in the humidicrib. Tubes and lines snaked in every direction, supplying oxygen, fluids and antibiotics. Monitors blinked and beeped. Bili lights to help lower the high bilirubin making Chloe's skin yellow, eerily highlighted the wee girl's predicament. The patch protecting her eyes added to the terrifying picture.

On Liz's other side Kevin looked as stunned and disbelieving as his wife sounded. 'She has to, Lizzie. She has to.'

Alex stepped around the incubator and checked

the oxygen flow. 'Liz, on a medical level you know she can. And yes, I know.' She sucked in an unsteady breath and ignored the fear for these two now making itself known in her chest. 'You're fully aware of all the things that can go wrong. I'm sure your heads are crammed with every scenario imaginable. Today you two are Mum and Dad, not doctors.' It must be dreadful for them. That precious little bundle held their hearts in her tiny, tiny hands. 'Hang on to the fact that babies thirty-two weeks premature do survive, more often than not with great outcomes.'

The eyes Liz turned on her were bleak. 'Gosh, Alex, how do we do that? It's so different standing on this side of the equation. You have no idea.'

Alex's mouth soured. Her eyes misted. *Oh, yes, I do. More than you can imagine. Worse, I know how it is when your baby dies.* But Chloe wasn't going to die. No way was Liz going to know the anguish of losing her child. *Not on my watch.* Her hands were shaking. She stuffed them deep into the pockets of her white coat, at the same time thrusting away a mental picture of holding

Jordan swathed in a tiny blanket as she pleaded for him to start breathing. *Come on, get a grip. This is about Liz and Kevin and their daughter, not you and your son.*

She sucked in air and winced as it touched the hole in her molar. 'I'm Chloe's doctor, sure, not her mum, so I'm not going through what you are. But believe me, I'll be doing everything within my power to help her.'

'As will I,' said a familiar, deep voice from somewhere above her shoulder. 'Chloe's got the A-team on her side.'

'Besides, Chloe's already shown us she's a fighter.' Alex risked a quick glance up at Mario and instantly wished she hadn't. He was watching her with a disturbing intensity that seemed to bore right inside to the place she kept her innermost secrets. She dropped her head, blinking away the telltale moisture at the corners of her eyes. Hopefully Mario hadn't noticed that. But somehow she knew he had. The man never missed anything.

Kevin cleared his throat. 'What about RDS?

That's always a possibility with her underdeveloped lungs.'

Alex had answered questions from Kevin and Liz about respiratory distress syndrome during the night, knew that they were well aware of the facts behind this condition common in prem babies. But they were beside themselves with worry and would ask the same questions again and again over the coming days and weeks. 'We're giving Chloe surfactant to help her lungs cope. As you know it keeps the air sacs open and allows better oxygen and carbon dioxide exchange.'

'I want to cuddle her to me,' Liz cried. 'It's not right that she can't be held by her mum and dad. She must be so lonely in there after all these months growing inside me.'

A shudder rocked Alex. That cry from Liz's heart was something she understood all too well. A hand touched hers briefly. Mario.

Kevin pulled Liz into his arms and rocked her, whispering into her ear, his face filled with distress.

Alex stepped aside, busying herself with checking monitors again, trying to ignore the ache in her own heart. Mario also moved away and joined her, flicking through Chloe's charts.

'Are you all right?' he murmured close to her ear.

Alex snapped straight. 'Of course. Why shouldn't I be? Apart from hurting for my friends, that is.' *Please don't ask me anything personal right now.*

His eyes met hers, locked gazes. 'You seem rattled.'

I am. Very. Think of something to say to divert that compassionate voice. Mario could so easily be the undoing of her carefully put-together life if she made a wrong move, said the wrong thing. 'Just as Liz and Kevin are struggling with being parents and not doctors with Chloe, I'm struggling with treating their child compared to a total stranger's baby. Not that I'll do anything different or with more effort, but I feel as though this case is different. I want Liz and Kevin to walk out of here one day with Chloe in their arms, heading for a bright future.'

Those pewter eyes didn't look away. But Mario's mouth softened into the warmest of smiles. 'I know exactly what you mean. It is harder when you know the patient's family personally. It shouldn't be but that's the way of it.'

Phew. She'd got away with shifting Mario's focus off her. Not that she hadn't been telling the truth, just not all the truth. 'Right, let's see if we can get these two to take a wee break and freshen themselves up.'

Mario headed for Sophia's room. Why did he get the feeling Alexandra was hiding something from him? From all of them? Was it to do with that sadness that often crept into her eyes when she thought no one was watching? He'd seen it a few times since they'd raced in here last night to work with Chloe. Back there when she'd told Liz she'd do anything possible for Chloe it had been as though she felt something more than a doctor did, felt a connection with Chloe's parents. Or did she just want—or was it need?—to prove she could save Chloe? Save Chloe unscathed from all the things that could go wrong?

'Hi, Daddy. Look what Alex gave me.' Sophia held up a different Harry and Bella book to the first one she'd received.

'Who's a lucky girl?'

'Me. Where's Alex?' Sophia leaned sideways in the bed to peer past him. 'Isn't she coming to see me?'

Mario chuckled. He'd thought Sophia would be thrilled so see him, but seems Alex ranked higher in the popularity stakes. 'Alexandra's looking after a very sick baby, but I'm sure she'll say hello later on. Do you want me to read you the new book?'

Sophia's head swung left, then right, left, then right, her eyes very solemn. 'Nope.'

Oh, okay. 'What about a game of snakes and ladders? Bet you can't beat me.'

'Course I can. Where's the board gone?' She leaned so far over the edge of the bed looking for it Mario grabbed her before she fell headfirst onto the floor.

'Careful, munchkins.' Mario settled down to entertain his daughter but his mind stayed with Alexandra and what might've upset her earlier.

Five games later he was none the wiser, but at least Sophia had settled down to rest. Her obs were good and if he hadn't needed to stay on overnight for Chloe he'd have taken her home. But Sophia was better off being here where he could spend time with her than going to Gina's and being trailed around rugby fields getting cold and tired. Besides, it was unfair to ask Gina to look after his child yet again.

Mario ran the back of his hand down his cheek. If only he had time to take the boys off her hands for a whole weekend and send her away to her girlfriend's for a night. But he barely managed to cope with his own hectic schedule. Which reminded him he needed to get to the supermarket or he and Sophia would be doing a starve when they got home. Maybe he could squeeze that in first thing tomorrow morning.

'Alex.' Sophia sat up, her eyes wide with excitement. 'Have you come to read me a story?'

'If that's what you want, little one.' Alex sat on the opposite side of the bed to him and smiled sweetly at his girl.

He didn't know whether to be amused or grateful that Sophia seemed to have taken such a shine to Alex. Not even with him had she been so accepting so fast. He'd never heard her ask anyone else to do something for her. Not even Gina. 'Blimey,' he muttered. Hopefully this wouldn't cause problems further down the track.

A warm hand covered his. 'You're her dad—you get to do all the hard work. I'm a novelty at the moment, probably because of the stories I write and she loves to hear.' Alexandra's fingers curled over his hand, squeezed lightly, then were withdrawn.

So she read his mind now? Scary thought. He'd have to be careful to only think about work when she was near. Looking at her, he found her smile now directed in his direction. 'So I'm not obsolete?' he asked in jest.

Instantly she turned serious. 'Your daughter adores you. She frets when she hasn't seen you for half an hour. She's always talking about you to anyone who'll listen.' An impish glint filtered into those fascinating eyes. 'Not that any of us stand around listening to all that nonsense.'

'It's good having my own cheerleader.'

Her gaze dipped. 'It must be.'

So she wasn't happy being alone. What was her history? She'd not mentioned a husband or children in any of their conversations. Not that Alexandra was good at talking about herself. Far from it. She lived alone now but had she ever been married? Did she have a family that now lived with an ex-partner? He knew so little about her and yet felt so at ease with her that he'd even spilled the beans about Sophia and Lucy.

'Daddy, are you going to listen to the story with us?' Sophia's high-pitched voice reminded him who was meant to be the centre of attention here.

Heat stole into Alexandra's cheeks. 'I think your daddy's got things to do.'

'Like lick my wounds after being thrashed at snakes and ladders.' Mario stood reluctantly. He'd love to stay and watch over Sophia and Alexandra, but he'd only make Alexandra uncomfortable. 'I'm going to look in on Chloe. I'll be back soon, sweetheart.'

'Okay, Daddy.'

Mario strode briskly out of the room trying to work out which of those two females he was calling sweetheart.

* * *

'How many times has Chloe stopped breathing?' Alexandra asked.

Mario read back to Jackson the measure of drug he was about to administer to his tiny patient, then turned to her. 'She's having regular apnoeic episodes, hence the methylanthine drug.'

'And I thought she was doing so well.' Alexandra stared down at the very small baby. 'Any sign of bradycardia with the apnoea?'

'Unfortunately, yes. And hypoxia.'

Alexandra's mouth tightened. 'Liz and Kevin must be beside themselves.'

Kay told her, 'It took some persuasion from Mario to get them to go downstairs for a coffee break together. They need time out.'

Mario expanded, 'They're exhausted. But who can blame them for wanting to be with Chloe every minute of the day and night. I know I wouldn't be able to leave her if she was mine.'

Jackson's pager interrupted. 'Looks like I'm needed elsewhere. I'll be back as soon as possible.'

Alexandra told him, 'Take a break when you can. I'll stay with Chloe for a while.'

'Me too,' Mario added, and settled on a chair

by the humidicrib to take yet another reading of Chloe's respiration movements, heart rate and pulse oximetry.

Sadness tugged at him for this girl and her parents. He thought he had problems with Sophia but at least she was healthy most of the time, except for the asthma. One day she'd overcome her past and then hopefully her ailment would clear up—a little at least.

Alexandra stood on the other side of the humidicrib, gazing at Chloe. 'It's so frightening how fragile life is.'

'Chloe's not giving up though.' The resp movements were slow.

'Amazing how hard these babies fight to survive. As though they understand what they have to do.' Alexandra sighed. 'I guess parents never really expect something like this to happen to their child.'

He filled in Chloe's chart and hooked it on the end of the crib. 'We're all optimists. Then again, I never knew I was going to be a dad so no worrying for me.' His lungs filled on a long intake of air. 'What about you? Ever think about having children?'

Her hands slipped into her coat pockets, her face clouded and those green eyes turned the shade of a forest. Still watching Chloe her chest rose and fell. 'No, I'm never having a family. I'm single for starters.'

'You wouldn't have one on your own?' Why was he pressing her? What made him want to know when they could never be more than friends at the most?

'I don't think that's fair on a kid. Anyway, I'm too involved in my career to give a child all the attention it needs, with or without a partner. I've got goals to attain.' But the eyes that finally met his didn't look so positive about that being a great idea.

If Alexandra thought she'd convinced him her career was all important she could think again. He was reluctant to ask any more though. She'd likely tell him to mind his own business. One thing he had learned was to approach her slowly, slowly. But the devil in him just had to add, 'Never say never. I can see you with a brood of your own, reading bedtime stories about dogs and dancing in the lounge to off-key singing.'

She shrugged. 'You really haven't heard my—' she waggled her forefingers in the air '—singing.'

He laughed. 'Apparently that's a good thing.' At least she hadn't bitten his head off. If only he knew how to banish that longing lurking in her eyes every time she looked at Chloe. Not for a second did he believe she didn't want children. Her career was an excuse. Every time he learned something new about Alexandra he found another brick wall to knock down.

Mathew stood in the doorway of Chloe's room as though blocking entrance to Mario and Alex. 'Go, the pair of you. Get some sleep. We've got it covered here.'

'Yes, and take Sophia out for some fun.' Jenny added her two cents' worth.

Alex looked at Mario and chuckled. 'Guess we've got our marching orders, then.' It was two weeks since Chloe's sudden and early birth and the tiny girl was doing well. Mathew had stepped in when needed to give them a break over that time.

Mario shrugged those wide shoulders that drove her to distraction. 'You are the boss.'

'You know what? I'm happy to step aside for a few hours.' And she had an idea of how to fill in her afternoon. She'd go out to her beach cottage and walk along the water's edge for an hour or so. But as she studied the man who'd kept her lying awake most of the few hours she'd got to spend in bed since that Friday two weeks ago when they'd nearly kissed, loneliness caught at her. That unforgettable near kiss had rattled her. If the hospital hadn't phoned at that moment would they've only kissed? Or would they've ended up in her enormous bed making hot love?

Sometime since then Alex had come to her senses. She worked with Mario. She was his HOD and had to keep the upper hand with him for those times that would arise when she had to speak sharply to him. Besides, he already had a messed-up child to sort out. He didn't need a messed-up woman as well.

So, no hot kisses, no lovemaking. Which didn't

make her happy at all. No, now she felt deprived of something special, wonderful, exciting. Heaven knew there wasn't a lot of excitement in her life these days. Only medical emergencies and they left her drained and worried, not light and happy, or exhilarated.

Today in body-snug jeans and a thick navy jersey covered by a woodsman jacket he was still as mouth-watering as he had been in dress trousers and shirt that night. Face it, Mario Forelli was a turn-on, and probably would be even if he appeared in Spiderman's costume.

She heard him asking, 'What do you think you'll do with your enforced time off?'

Hide out at the cottage and try to find the Alex of a few weeks ago. The one who remained in control of her emotions no matter what. The one who definitely did not get excited over a man. Not any man. This man. Her mind and body could do with some quiet time. Her mouth had other ideas. 'Going for a walk on the beach. Want to join me?'

'I'd have to bring Sophia.'

'I expect you to.' Sophia's presence would act

as a buffer between them. Just in case things heated up again. Which they mustn't.

'So where are we going? Tahunanui Beach or further afield?'

'Ruby Bay.' When Mario's eyes scrunched in question she enlightened him. 'I've got a cottage right on the beach that I inherited from my father. It's where we all came every summer for a month over Christmas and New Year.' It's where she learned to swim. Where dad used to take her fishing in his small alloy boat or put out a net overnight. The place where, weather permitting, all meals were outdoors and all the neighbours gathered round at the end of the day to share a barbecue.

Her mother had been against her inheriting the cottage but Alex had stood up to her mother, fighting for what she wanted. In a way her dad was still there for her, sometimes making her smile, sometimes causing her to weep.

'Bet you have lots of wonderful memories from then,' Mario said.

'Absolutely. It's my favourite place in the whole wide world for that reason.' It had also been her bolthole over the years. It was the place she'd grieved after losing her son. This was where she'd tried to come to terms with Jonty's defection. The cottage and the beach were filled with sweet and harsh memories. Those memories were what her life was made of. The good and the bad. The losses. The things that had crushed her heart so badly she'd never risk sharing it again—no matter how tempting a man like Mario was. No one was worth that intense, excruciating pain. She'd never survive the relentless, burning agony another time. No point even considering it could be different next time. She'd thought that once and learned how wrong she could be. All her life she'd lost those she loved—one way or another.

'Then you're lucky to have such a place.'

Mario stood at the bay window, breathing in the relaxing atmosphere of Alexandra's special place. Surprising that she'd invited him here, really. This was showing him more about her than any conversation had so far in their relationship.

You don't have a relationship with Alexandra.

Other than a working one. And one meal and an almost kiss at her apartment.

On the beach young boys kicked a ball along the wet sand, shouting as though the world was deaf, and having a wonderful time. If only Sophia felt confident enough to join in but as usual she'd stayed glued to his side when they'd ventured to the bottom of the lawn. Now she was sitting at the table reading a Harry and Bella book. Whatever, she was happy and so was he. 'This is so magical.' He sighed. 'I feel like I've been transported to another planet. The hospital and all those sick youngsters seem a long way away.'

Alexandra paused her lunch preparations and came to stand beside him, instantly distracting him with the scent of the outdoors overlaid with pine smoke from her woodchippy that burned in the corner of the room. 'It has that effect on me too.'

Turning slightly he watched, fascinated, as her mouth curved into a gentle smile. Without thought he leaned closer, traced a finger along that smile, felt her lips stretch wider and open slightly under his fingertip, drawing him into her heat. Her tongue touched, licked. He tried backing away, couldn't, his feet apparently nailed to the floor.

That unfinished kiss lay between them. It was in her shy glances when she didn't think he was watching her, in her guarded smiles. It fizzed along his veins, fried his brain. It would not be denied any longer. So tilting her head up with his hand under her chin he lowered his mouth to hers. Where this would take them he didn't know, didn't question. He just had to have his fill of her. Now. He tasted her. And couldn't get enough. His tongue pressed into her mouth, further, deeper. Savouring, exploring. The world spun away, leaving him alone with Alexandra. Nothing, no one else, mattered.

Her hands laced at the back of his neck, pulled him down to her level, brought him closer to her warm body. Her return kiss was fierce, laden with sweetness, passion, desire. For him. He breathed her in—her feminineness, her hair, her skin, her heated body.

He had to touch that skin, to feel her under his palms. A quick tug freed her shirt from her trousers. Sliding his hands underneath the soft fabric he touched her silky skin. Hot. Smooth. Tormenting.

She moaned against his mouth.

He hardened instantly. A fast takeoff. They'd only moments ago been talking, not kissing. And now he was ready. Throbbing. For Alexandra. He needed to sink into her. To know all of her.

His mouth still possessing hers, Mario lifted Alexandra up against him, pressed her body the length of his. His arousal pushed against her stomach.

Another moan escaped her lips. He opened his eyes to watch the emotions flickering across her face. Desire matching his had turned the green of her eyes deeper, darker, so that he felt he was tipping into bottomless pools.

Alexandra turned her head, and stilled. 'Mario,' she whispered.

His mouth followed hers, intent on furthering the kiss. *Don't interrupt me. Not now. I can't bear to stop.*

'Mario.' Her tone became insistent.

His eyes nearly disappeared as he struggled to

look around while continuing to kiss this goddess. All those dreams since that night in her apartment hadn't come close to the real thing. Kissing Alexandra was now his favourite pastime.

'We have an audience.'

Blink. Who? Slowly he pulled his mouth away from those delicious lips. Great. The boys with the ball were now lined up at the edge of the lawn, laughing and pointing up to him and Alexandra. 'Go away,' he muttered without rancour. Sliding Alexandra down his body he settled her on her feet, wishing he never had to let her go again. Which was a very good reason to drop his hands to his sides.

Alexandra's laugh was rough, filled with tension and wonder as she turned away. 'I'd better finish getting lunch ready before Sophia starts wanting food.'

How did she do that? Walk away from that kiss? Wasn't she burning up inside? He was. He'd swear she felt the same.

'Mario, where's Sophia?'

'What?' A bucket of icy water poured over

his head wouldn't have dampened his ardour as quickly. 'Sophia?' He spun to gape at the empty chair at the table. 'Sophia.'

'It's all right. She won't have gone far.'

He shook Alexandra's hand from his arm. 'She's probably hiding. It's what she does when no one's looking. And then she has an asthma attack.' What if she'd witnessed him kissing Alexandra? That would send her crawling into a dark corner to avoid him.

'Mario,' Alexandra spoke sharply. 'Calm down. We'll find her. She can't have gone far in that time.'

Alex watched Mario stride across to the door leading outside, tossing angry words over his shoulder at her. 'Easy for you to say. You don't what it's like to lose your child.'

'Yes, I do,' she whispered. Pain laced her words. Gone was the desire from moments ago. Replaced with a hideous memory. *Yes, Mario, I know exactly what it's like to lose your child, to hold them close when there's no hope. To scream silently with pain, with despair, longing. To be filled with love and words that you can no longer give. To fall into an abyss where pain was shelved until you peeked out into reality again. I know the reality more than you do.*

Outside Mario yelled at the top of his lungs, 'Sophia, where are you?'

Alex watched him go, saw him peering down the beach, left, then right, left, then right, undecided on which direction to take. Thank goodness he hadn't heard her secret. They might be getting close, too close, but no way did she want to share Jordan with him.

'Sophia, stop hiding and come to Daddy.'

Mario's urgency snapped Alex out of her own pain. 'I'll search inside the cottage first.'

Again he didn't hear her, but she made sure he heard her a minute later when she ran to the door and yelled, 'Mario, it's all right. Sophia's inside.'

He spun around to race back to the cottage. 'Where? Is she safe?' Mario sped past her, his eyes wild with worry. 'Where's my girl? I need to see her, to make sure nothing's wrong.'

'She's having fun.'

Reaching for his hand Alex pulled him to a

halt. 'She's as happy as any child can be.' She put her finger to her lips. 'Shh. Come quietly.' And she led him down the hall to her studio.

At the doorway she stopped and pushed Mario through so he could see Sophia. The little girl had climbed up onto the stool in front of the artist's pad where a nearly completed page for a new Harry and Bella book was pinned to a board. She was leaning forward, her little face scrunched up as her finger traced along the words she was trying to enunciate.

'"Bella is hiding Harry's far—"' She leaned so close she surely couldn't see the word. 'Bella is hiding something.' Lifting her head she used her forefinger to carefully outline the pencilled picture of Bella digging a hole under a lemon tree.

Mario turned back to Alex. Relief glittered out at her. 'I'm sorry. I guess I overreacted but—' He stopped, swiped a hand through his hair. 'She terrifies me whenever she disappears. I don't know what's going on in her mind. She underlines the fact I haven't a clue what happened in the years she wasn't mine that makes her do this.'

'Stay with her, read the words aloud.' She

wanted to reach out and hold him, smooth away that pain twisting his mouth, staining his eyes. She even took a step towards him, stopped when he tensed up, as unyielding as a concrete wall. Despite what he'd just told her he didn't want her touch, wouldn't let her share the burden. Well, that was something she understood, something they had in common. 'I'll get you a coffee.'

'Her mother didn't want her.' His eyes filled with fury and agony. 'How could any woman not want her child? Lucy carried Sophia in her belly for nine months. Wouldn't she have formed a bond with her baby in that time?'

Yes. Definitely. Alex opened her mouth in response, but closed it as his flood of words continued.

'I never would've believed Lucy incapable of loving Sophia. She wasn't always affectionate or outwardly loving with me but I thought that was because of a fairly loveless upbringing. But shouldn't that have made her try harder? Then when she chose not to bring Sophia up shouldn't she have brought my daughter to me? She never gave me a chance.'

'She still didn't tell you even when Sophia was born?'

'Nope. Not a word. One day we were living in Florence, planning for our wedding, the next she'd gone. It wasn't until I bumped into a colleague from our training days in London and was shunned that I finally learned I'd apparently tossed Lucy out when she became pregnant to me, and that Lucy had died. I immediately began searching for my child.'

'The six missing months in your CV.'

'No.' Mario turned to head down the hall. Getting away from little ears? 'Those happened once I'd found her in foster care about to be adopted by her most recent carers. She'd been through the mill—her mother's desertion, three different foster families, the asthma, nightmares about God knows what. All by the time she was three.'

A quick glance at Sophia showed her still totally engrossed in Harry and Bella so Alex followed Mario, quietly, letting him vent, barely able to comprehend Sophia's life. Totally unable to understand the girl's mother. What Lucy'd done was unforgivable. In the kitchen she reached for the coffee maker and spooned in grinds.

Mario had plonked his butt down on a bar stool by the kitchen island. 'I met Lucy while specialising in London. She'd gone over there to study at Oxford and we were at the same party one night. Hit it off immediately. But when I moved to Florence things started going awry. Lucy swore my family didn't like her and that they made her life difficult whenever she came to stay with me.' Lifting a glass of water he drank deeply. 'She might've had a point. There are a lot of Forellis, and we can be full-on, especially when you're an only child from small-town New Zealand.'

Alex gulped. She'd do well to remember that. Just in case she ever got to meet any of Mario's family. 'I would've said it could be daunting for an only child from the middle of anywhere.'

'You're probably right.' His smile flicked on, then off. 'I still believed we were in love and getting married once she'd finished her degree, until the day she sent me a note saying she was going to the Caribbean and I wasn't invited. Oh, and that she wouldn't be back. End of engagement.'

'That's harsh.' And cruel. Mario must've been devastated. If the way he was with Sophia was anything to go by he loved deeply, and having Lucy dump him so carelessly would've been dreadful for him.

'To say the least.' His throat worked as he swallowed more water. 'Then one day I learned Lucy had been pregnant and I began tracking her down, only to find she'd died while scuba diving and that there was a child back in England. Finally after a lot of door knocking, welfare desk thumping and a DNA test I found Sophia.'

'It's unbelievable. I don't understand why Lucy wouldn't tell you about your daughter. Especially as it seems she didn't want her. She'd have known your family would've taken Sophia in, surely?' Mind-boggling, to say the least. Alex shook her head. She'd never have deserted her child, no matter what the situation.

'Probably payback for how she perceived they'd treated her. Looking back I can see that Lucy was very selfish. She did tell me she wasn't ready to have a family but I thought she'd get past that when we were married. Seems I was wrong. But

I have to take some of the blame, I guess. I was working all hours, putting my career before all else.'

'Sophia's lucky you found her. You might think she's got a way to go but she loves you so much. That's a huge step forward considering everything she must've been through.'

'I quit my job in Florence and spent months living near to Sophia, letting her get used to me before I pulled her out of her foster home she'd got used to and brought her halfway around the world to start yet again.'

'She's very lucky you found her,' Alex repeated.

'Yeah,' he sighed. Suddenly out of words? 'Yeah. I hope so.'

'Give yourself time.'

'Now you know why my life is totally dedicated to Sophia. I could've returned to Florence and my relatives but she'd have had to learn Italian and that wasn't fair when she was barely coping with almost everything going on in her life. Also I had a fantastic childhood here and wanted that for my child. It seemed the right thing to do, still does most of the time.' His smile was ironic.

'That's why I'm living and working in Nelson. And why I'm living the life of a monk.'

Alex felt her eyebrows rising. Too much information? Or a warning? 'So monks kiss, then?'

That beautiful mouth twitched, then a full-on laugh rumbled over his bottom lip. 'Touché.'

CHAPTER EIGHT

ALEX FINISHED HER last patient round and handed over to the night shift. 'Hope you have a quiet night,' she told Jenny, barely swallowing a yawn. Chloe had taken a backward step at two in the morning and Alex hadn't been home since.

'Not a chance.' The nurse dropped files into a tray. 'Mario's still in theatre operating on the little girl with post meningitis complications.'

Alex winced. 'He's amputating Bee Harvey's legs now? I thought that was scheduled for this morning.' It should've been done and the child back on the ward by now.

'Theatre got taken over with an emergency. An MVA with multiple casualties which threw the operating list into complete disarray. Mario opted to operate late rather than put the girl's parents through any more distress waiting for it to happen another day.' Jenny dropped onto her chair.

'Not that they're going to feel any better about the operation's outcome. Their beloved little girl is still going to have to learn to walk all over again.'

Alex nibbled her lip. 'Absolutely ghastly for them all. I can't even begin to imagine what they must be going through.' But she did know how Mario would be feeling when he finally finished his hideous task and spoke to the parents. He'd be gutted, sad and, being a dad, terrified of something similar ever happening to Sophia. 'So who's looking after Sophia, do you know?'

'Mario left her in the hospital day care centre until Gina could pick her up when she finished her shift. How those two manage their families is beyond me. Which reminds me, there's pasta in the fridge for Mario to take home that one of the ED nurses dropped in.'

A smile broke through Alex's gloom. 'That guy doesn't know how lucky he is with all of you running around after him.'

'Who wouldn't want to spoil that gorgeous little girl?' When Alex raised her eyebrows at that Jenny laughed. 'Yeah, all right. He's so hot no one's going to let him go hungry. In more ways than one—except he's not obliging any of the girls in that way.'

At least she'd had his kisses. And so far hadn't paid for it with food. 'Call me if anything crops up, especially if Chloe's condition changes. I'm not expecting trouble. Which is a very silly thing to have said. I'll drop in to check on her later tonight.' She crossed her fingers against her thigh. 'And leave Mario alone tonight unless it's about his patient.'

'Will do, though I think he's sleeping over anyway to be here for Bee.' Jenny made a note for the staff and then lifted the ringing phone.

Alex's next stop was her office. Except she didn't know why. Unless she could blame this strange restlessness gripping her, making her feel as though she'd been blindfolded and turned around and around until she was dizzy. Right now she should be driving home, stopping to get something for dinner on the way. Not sitting in her office staring round like she'd never seen this room before. Another ward round before she left? Looking for Mario? Seeing if he'd finished in theatre yet?

Go home, Alex. Be sensible.

It was the 'be sensible' that did it, sending her delving into the phone book and looking up a restaurant to order an appropriate dinner for two to eat in a staff kitchenette off the ward at whatever hour Mario felt it safe to leave his wee patient.

The 'be sensible' tolling in her head had her warring with herself about how it was time to stop being sensible about absolutely everything in her life. It was all very well to play life safe, not endanger her heart, nor leap into a relationship without checking the water, but sometimes, just sometimes, it was very tempting to step outside the boundaries she'd erected around her life.

Define *sometimes.*

I've never done it before.

Umm, what about that very short fling last year?

A blip on an otherwise clean and clear lifestyle. Boring.

What's to say Mario won't turn out to be a similar blip?

Because I don't want him to.

Alex gasped at her own honesty. But unfortunately Mario had pretty much said there was no room for anyone else in his life while he concentrated on getting Sophia through to adulthood.

'Asian Gardens Restaurant. How can I help?'

Alex gave up arguing with herself and ordered dinner for two to be ready for her to collect in an hour's time. She was no different to all the other females working in the hospital.

Mario rolled his shoulders, stretched his back, then tossed his cap into the basket, and patted his rumbling stomach. 'Quiet.'

Bee Harvey lay in recovery, slowly being brought round to a drug controlled, semi-comatose state. It was too soon for reality.

Reality: a world where her legs below her knees were gone. At six years old it seemed preposterous what she was facing. She'd already been through hell. The meningitis had taken its toll, leaving her thin, fragile and at risk of more rampant infections. What he'd done to her, for her, broke his heart. Right now he loathed his job. All very well to say someone had to do it. He hadn't met a doctor yet who'd say they were happy to amputate a child's legs—no matter what the circumstances.

Wandering into recovery he stood for a quiet moment, watching over Bee as she fought waking up. He wanted her to stay asleep, unaware of her future. Realistically, at her age it would take some time for the full force of her operation to hit home. But it would hit hard one day. No avoiding that. Especially once she was ready to join her friends, return to school, to go to birthday parties, play sport. At least she had good, caring parents to help her through it all. With a bit of luck thrown in her head space wouldn't be screwed.

'Her obs are good,' the nurse assigned to Bee told him.

He nodded, resisting the urge to lean over and kiss the child's forehead. Just. An image slipped into his mind of Sophia looking totally bewildered when he first took her away from her foster home. Instantly he wanted to be at home, holding his girl.

But there'd be no going home tonight. He was staying here, ready at a moment's notice if something went wrong for Bee. He might lie down on the hard cot and close his eyes, he might even doze off, but he'd be on full alert if he was needed.

Slowly he headed for the washroom where he tossed his soiled scrubs into a laundry basket and pulled on a clean set. He wrenched a tap on full force, splashed cold water over his face, trying to sluice the ache and grit from his eyes and mouth. Shaking his head he leaned forward, his hands gripping the basin, and stared into the mirror before him.

A weary man stared back. A man with a million questions about his life zipping out of those cool, cloudy eyes. Almost a stranger. When had he got so exhausted, so unsure of what he was doing with his life? Bringing Sophia home had been the right thing to do and he didn't regret that at all.

In doing so he'd dropped his ambition to be at the top of the world of paediatrics and surprisingly that hadn't been as hard as he'd expected. The career he'd always dreamt of, had worked hard for. The career that had destroyed his relationship with Lucy, and what he'd wanted more than anything up until a year ago when he'd learned he was a father.

He'd also given up any hope of more family of his own, of a wife or partner to share the highs and lows with. At least he had until Alexandra Prendergast arrived in his life.

All his certainty turned to dust in his mouth. Now he glimpsed something he might want to grab for the future, to hold on to and cherish. A life, a family, a woman who tipped him upside down with a word. With a kiss.

Cupping his hands, he filled them with water to pour over his head, letting it trickle down his cheeks, his neck, into his clothes. It didn't take away the fog in his skull, didn't provide answers to all the questions pestering him non-stop. Pulling in a lungful of air he headed for the ward.

'How did Bee's surgery go?' Alex looked up from the nurses' computer as Mario approached. Heck, the guy's eyes were dull with exhaustion. His shoulders had dropped and his walk was slow. He needed taking care of. Someone to prepare him a hot bath and give him a massage. Make a meal and pour a glass of his favourite red wine.

'Straightforward. Poor little tyke.' A yawn stretched that delicious mouth.

Alex gulped at the closeness of that wide chest. If she leaned ever so slightly sideways she could lay her cheek against it and hear his heart beating and know his strength. She jerked the other way, and nearly tipped off the chair.

'Easy.' Mario caught her arm, helped her regain her balance.

Blushing profusely she straightened her back, looked along the ward to avoid meeting his all-seeing gaze. 'Thanks,' she muttered, and rapidly changed the subject. 'You could ask me to sleep over.' Heat flamed in her cheeks. Not what she meant at all.

His fingers slashed through his wet hair. 'I could.' Then he smiled. '*Grazie*. But I'm fine, really.'

Standing, Alex touched his arm lightly. 'Come with me.'

'What now? Another patient you want me to see? Chloe?'

Shaking her head, she repeated, 'Come with me,' and headed towards the kitchenette. If only she had an oven in her office, then this could've been a more intimate moment.

He didn't immediately follow her. *Do I have to grab him and haul his body down the ward? Or should I bring the meal to him at the nurses' station?* Suddenly her certainty that she'd been doing the right thing for Mario evaporated. Doubt at her ability to read men and their needs reared up. Why couldn't he just have done as she'd asked?

'Where are you taking me?' Mario spoke from directly behind her.

Phew. Her mouth relaxed into a wide smile. 'Wait and see.' When she turned into the kitchenette she glanced over her shoulder and saw relief fill his eyes. 'Relax, this isn't about a patient.'

Mario closed the door behind them. Shutting work out for a short while? His shoulder leaned into the wall, his feet crossed at the ankles. And he sniffed the air. 'Please tell me you've got food in here.'

Placing plates and cutlery on the table Alex said, 'I hope you like Thai.'

'Bring it on.' He stared at her, his mouth relaxing at last. 'You're serious, aren't you?'

She began removing containers from a heated bag and opening lids. 'Phad Thai, chicken green curry, prawn fried rice, beef salad, fish cakes.'

'This is a banquet. Who else is joining us?' He pushed off the wall and held a chair out for her.

'I tried to cover all the options.' Looking at the mountain of food on the tiny table she shook her head. She'd gone overboard, as bad as the girls who brought in casseroles for him. 'I guess the night shift will make short work of what we don't eat.'

Mario took a seat beside her. Not opposite, but next to her. Picking up a spoon he hesitated and looked at her. 'Thank you. I need this. The food, the distraction from Bee, your company.'

'I know.' At least she knew about the first two, but her company? That was a surprise. 'It's been a grim day for you.'

Leaning closer his mouth brushed her lips. 'Yeah, but it's looking up.'

Warmth stole through her and she pressed her mouth against his. His lips curved tantalisingly against hers before he pulled away.

'At the risk of insulting you I think I'd better eat. If I continue that kiss, then this food will get cold. And anyone could barge in on us at any moment. I don't think you'd like your staff seeing you kiss one of your specialists.' The smile didn't falter, and the warmth in his eyes grew, letting her know he wasn't trying to avoid her, just keeping their places at work in order.

Picking up a fork Alex began filling her plate with a little bit of everything. She really would've liked more of that kiss. Even here at work where they could be interrupted. She'd have dealt with it. Surprise caught her. Yes, she would've. Definitely stepping outside her safety net.

The first mouthful of curry sent exotic flavours bursting through her mouth. 'Oh, yes, that's so delicious.' When she glanced at Mario he was staring at her, a smile on his beautiful mouth. 'What?'

He swallowed. Leaned over and kissed her

cheek. 'This is great.' Then he concentrated on eating, filling his plate twice.

Voices, hurrying footsteps, laughter from the ward, filtered through into the kitchen, wrapping round them, making it unnecessary to talk, letting them be comfortable with each other.

Alex had no idea where this was going, or if there even was anything between her and Mario, but she didn't care. For once she was happy to let whatever it was play out in its own good time.

Except she'd give an arm to kiss Mario again. Just thinking it made the air sizzle. She'd swear she heard the crackle of sparks as she watched this intriguing man doing something as simple as enjoying a meal. Except it wasn't simple. Every time they were together without the benefit of other people to keep them on the straight and narrow Alex knew this deep pull in her belly. A longing, a need, that would not be denied. No matter how crazy the notion might seem to her 'sensible' side she wanted Mario. Not just his kiss but all of him—his skin against her body, his hands stroking, exploring her. His arousal pressing into her, entering her.

The door opened and Jenny sauntered in. 'Nice for some.' She nodded at the remaining food, carefully avoiding looking at Alex's hand near Mario's. 'Mario, Bee is back in her room. Her temp is slightly elevated, and she's restless.'

Shoving his chair back, Mario unwound his frame and stood. 'I'll be right there.' He began clearing the table, rinsing his plate in the sink. 'I'll give her more pain relief and keep her sedated for the night.'

'Leave those.' Alex took a container out of his hands. 'Go and see to your patient. Jenny, tell everyone to help themselves to what's left.'

At the door Mario turned back. 'Go home and take a break, Alexandra. The ward doesn't need both of us dropping with exhaustion.'

'Yes, sir.' But she smiled. And went home.

Mario turned off the motor and sat for a moment, letting the cold night air sharpen his mind. Was he about to make a huge mistake? Through the windscreen he studied the stars but they had no answers for him. He'd have to rely on his gut instinct.

And that said, *Run*.

But he'd never been a coward.

Out on the roadside he hesitated again. When Alexandra had brought dinner in for him two nights ago he'd had to admit he'd been humbled at her thoughtfulness. Since then he'd tormented himself with questions about why she'd done that. Because she was a kind woman? Because she was treating him specially? The second idea suited him better. And fitted in with that sizzling moment that would've led to another hot kiss if Jenny hadn't burst in on them.

He looked up at the apartment block towering above him. Lights from Alexandra's lounge shone bright against the dark of the rest of the building. Unable to sleep? It was past midnight and she should be tucked up in dreamland.

So should he. But the dreams he'd have would be X-rated and only serve to wind him ever tighter. And he'd only shared a kiss with her. Alexandra was something else. Which was a problem because he couldn't imagine not getting to know her better—in every way possible.

He tossed the keys in the air, caught them,

tossed them, caught them. Pushed them into his pocket and strode to the entrance of the apartment building. Lifting the speaker phone he pressed the button.

'Hello?' Wariness croaked out at him.

'Alexandra, it's me, Mario. I know it's late but I would like to see you.' *I'd like to hold you, kiss you, make love to you.* Swallowing hard in a hopeless attempt to squash down the lump of need blocking his throat he waited. Surely she'd tell him to get lost. At this hour who could blame her?

Buzz. The lock clicked. One quick push and he was inside, striding for the lift, which took him to the top floor all too quickly.

And there she was, standing in her doorway, wearing another shapeless tracksuit, her feet covered with fluffy socks, her hair floating around her shoulders.

It was the hair that did it. He'd spent days and nights wondering how that thick auburn hair would look when set free of its usual constraints. Shining waves tumbled around her face, highlighting her elfin features, framing those pull-him-in eyes.

Words deserted him. His fingers slid down her hair, then through the curls, lifting strands, inhaling the lemony scent of her shampoo. Heat pooled in his gut. Expanded his chest. Sent his blood south.

'Mario?' Alexandra whispered.

'Shh.' His arms encompassed her, brought her lithe frame against his bigger one. So delicate, yet not fragile. Lifting her against him he stepped into her apartment and kicked the door shut with a resounding clunk.

Those big green eyes got bigger as they filled with desire. For him. That sensual mouth curved wickedly, tantalisingly. Dainty hands slid around his neck and fixed her body firmly to his. Any last shred of restraint disappeared.

How had they got down the hall to the dining room so quickly? Dining room? They needed a bedroom. The woman in his arms stood on the tops of his shoes and stretched as tall as she could to fix her lips to his. Sweet hell, she tasted of— woman. Hot woman. Alexandra. A groan ripped through him, across his lips into their kiss.

Bedroom. Now. Dining room? Table. Ah-ha.

He walked them across the carpet up to the enormous, highly polished Rimu table. Backing Alexandra against the edge he held her tight while his mouth devoured hers. Her tongue darted across his bottom lip. His belly cramped as the desire increased, winding tighter and tighter until he was about to explode.

Alexandra shuffled her bottom against the table. Her fingers were working his belt and buckle, his zip. And then his manhood was free, sliding against the warm flesh of her palms. Jerking his mouth away from hers he tried to gain some control. His chest rose and fell sharply as he hauled air into his lungs. 'Alex? We need to slow down.'

She blinked, smiled fast and hot and so sexy. 'We do?'

'Okay, maybe not,' he croaked. 'You're sure about this?' If she wasn't he was in big trouble.

'Yes.' That beautiful mouth kissed a trail over his chin, around his neck to his ear. Her teeth bit his earlobe, sending him past stopping. Reaching between them he was stunned to find her lower half already naked. When had that happened?

In his arms Alexandra was turning her back to him, bending so that her buttocks pushed back against his erection. Leaning forward over the table her hands searching between his legs, finding him, squeezing gently, rolling his balls carefully between finger and thumb.

'Wait,' he managed to gasp. 'Condom.' He groped in his pocket for his wallet, hoping the condom hadn't fallen out over the months since he'd put it there. Haste made getting it on difficult but finally he managed and reached for her moist nub, rubbed long and slow.

Almost instantly her back arched as she shuddered against his hand. Quick, sharp pants and she was guiding him into her. Mario gasped at the wet heat enveloping his shaft. And then the sensations blasting through him took over and he ascended the pinnacle to fall over the edge. With Alexandra.

Alex twisted her head on the pillow and in the weak light from the hallway she studied the man lying next to her as warmth and laughter bubbled along her veins. Amazing. The man was amazing. So big, yet incredibly tender. 'Hey,' she whispered. 'How're you doing over there?'

'Couldn't be better.' He rolled onto his side and draped an arm over her waist, pulled her closer, kissed the top of her head, making her feel unusually cherished.

Snuggling closer, her lips tracked a line down his chest to his bellybutton where her tongue made slick circles. She'd made love with Mario. Twice. And each time had been better than she could've ever imagined. Not because it had been a while, but because he'd made her feel like a goddess in the way he touched her body with his hands, his tongue, his eyes.

Tension squeezed her. Thank goodness that in the heat of the moment she hadn't tossed her sweatshirt off in the full glare of the dining room lights. Then she'd be answering some difficult questions right about now. Just as well that in here the sheets covered her stomach and breasts. When Mario had tried to tug them away from her she played shy. Guilt at that was fleeting. Tonight was not the time to be telling Mario her life story. That time might never come. It was hard to show anyone her vulnerable side, especially after Jonty hadn't taken her seriously, had accused her of dramatising everything.

'Hello, Alexandra, where've you gone?' His fingers stroked her spine. 'You've left me.'

Perceptive, huh? 'Just languishing in the afterglow.'

Deep in his chest she heard the rumble of his laugh begin. 'I'm not a rocket.'

'You certainly take off on a hurry.'

'That—' he tapped her nose with a forefinger '—is your fault for being so desirable. It would've been a sin to have ignored you.' His lips brushed her forehead. 'You're one hot lady, Alexandra Prendergast.'

As her name slid off his tongue like warm syrup Alex stretched her legs towards the bottom of the bed, luxuriating in being so close to him, in the feel of a man beside her, his hip touching hers, his thigh against her leg. This was something she didn't have in her life, and until now hadn't realised was missing. With the few other men she'd slept with over the years she'd always wanted her bed back to herself once they'd finished having sex. But tonight she wanted to tie Mario to the mattress, keep him there to have her wicked way with him whenever the fancy grabbed her. Even better would be to wake up beside him in the morning. Scary.

As though he'd read her mind he sat up and swung his legs over the edge of the bed. 'I'd better be going home. It wouldn't do for someone from work seeing me leaving here in the morning.'

Disappointment throbbed loud in her ears. She hadn't finished with him. Would she ever be? 'The odds on that happening are small.'

'You want to risk it? Really? I know I don't.'

Feeling at a disadvantage lying flat on her back while Mario gazed down at her she hurriedly slid up the bed to lean against the headboard, making sure the sheet didn't slip below her breasts. 'I guess that depends on where this is going.'

'Which brings us to why I turned up here tonight. Let me get my clothes first.'

Watching him stride out of her bedroom a sinking feeling of impending loss overtook all other emotions, dampening the warmth of sexual release, shutting down her hope that she and Mario might find a way to have a relationship and still work well together. Not wanting to hear him say this had been a mistake, especially while she lay in her rumpled bed that he'd help destroy, she leapt out of bed and grabbed her robe. Slipping into it she followed him down the hall.

Tugging his shirt over his head and smoothing it down that broad expanse of chest he looked thoughtful. Too thoughtful.

The thumping of her heart slowed. Two hours ago she hadn't believed there was a hope in hell she'd ever make love with Mario. Now she didn't want to lose the opportunity to do it again. The words to stall him, hold off whatever he was about to say, snagged around the lump in her throat. Her hands twined the belt of her robe round and round, wove it through her fingers.

Mario stepped in front of her, reached for her hands. 'I'd like to have an affair with you.'

CHAPTER NINE

AS ALEXANDRA'S EYES widened in surprise Mario cursed under his breath. How was that for finesse? Blunt didn't begin to describe it. But he'd been nervous. So totally out of character. But this was Alexandra and she did strange things to him. He kept holding her hands, could feel her trembling. 'I'm sorry. That didn't come out how I wanted it to.'

'You d-don't want an affair?' Her cheeks paled.

Hope rose through the mess in his head. '*Sì*, I do.' He couldn't resist placing a tender kiss on her mouth. 'Definitely.' Then quickly withdrew before he tossed her over his shoulder and headed back to her bedroom.

Her stance softened as relief flowed through her. 'Good.'

'Good? That's it?' His knuckles dragged down his face. He'd thought he'd have to spend hours convincing her and she just said good?

'Definitely good.' A smile twitched at the corners of her sweet mouth. 'I haven't had enough of you yet.'

'Alexandra.' Mario stepped further away, strode to the big window overlooking the harbour, spun back to lock gazes with her. 'I have to explain. It can only be an affair. Nothing else. I have Sophia's future to think about and I've already sworn to put her first in my life. At least until she's totally settled into her new life and the way that's going it could be years.'

Looking somewhere beyond his shoulder she replied, 'I'm not looking for a long-term relationship either. Just a little fun until it doesn't work for us any more. Until the heat burns out.'

'Then we understand each other.' Too well. So why did his heart ache? Why had his gut suddenly turned sour? He should be swinging from the light fittings. He was going to have a fling with this beautiful woman who turned him on with a look. Alexandra had brought him alive tonight, reminding him of what he'd been missing out on, of what certain parts of his body were for. He'd have the affair he wanted and in return intended giving Alexandra a wonderful experience. Yet it seemed all wrong.

Why had Alexandra agreed to this? He'd have sworn she'd want the full works: the shared house, the wedding, babies. Despite saying he'd put Sophia first and not bring anyone else into her messed-up life, yet he could no longer pretend he was happy with that edict. He wanted it all. He was thirty-five after all. If he'd listened to Mamma he'd already be married with a brood of kids rushing around his house. Of course all the girls she'd paraded past him hadn't snagged his attention. Not one of them had been anything like Alexandra.

Stop being greedy. Sophia's an angel. Alexandra's amazing, beautiful, sexy. Not to mention being his boss. He shrugged. So what? It wouldn't be the first time the boss had a fling with a colleague.

Shyly Alexandra asked, 'I guess this is to be kept quiet? No sneaking out my front door first thing in the morning?'

'I'm afraid so. Firstly, I need to go home to Sophia. The new nanny is a gem and having her live in Monday to Saturday is a bonus, but I still have to be there for my daughter. Secondly, I don't think it's a good idea that our colleagues know about this, do you?' He'd turned that question back on her, testing to see how far she was prepared to go in letting the world know about their arrangement.

'I guess not.' Her perfectly white teeth nibbled her bottom lip. 'So no hiding away in the ward's linen cupboard or locking my office door while we kiss each other senseless?'

Squelching the questions buzzing around his head he reached for this fabulous woman, wrapped her in his arms and held her tight. His chin rested on the top of her head, and he sniffed in the scent of her hair. 'We could press the fire alarm first, clear the place out.'

Alex wandered into work the next morning, late and in a daze. Mario's touch was imprinted on her skin giving her a sense of joy and excitement. How was she going to concentrate on little patients without vivid pictures of last night getting in the way?

And there he was. Talking to Jenny and Kay at handover, looking as though nothing out of the ordinary had happened. Maybe for him it hadn't. Maybe he was used to brain-melting, body-burning sex. Just then he raised his head and looked down the ward, directly at her.

Under her ribs her heart rolled over and put its feet in the air, waiting to be tickled. Yeah, right. Brain melt still in charge. But that man had to be the most handsome, sexy, gorgeous male on earth. Did she mention sexy? She wanted him. Now. Here. Anywhere. Anyhow. Where was the closest fire alarm? Cripes, as far as flings went this one was going to be stellar.

'Morning, Alexandra.' That honeyed voice rolled down the corridor straight to her tummy, turning her knees hopelessly weak.

'Mario.' She dipped her head, running her tongue across her lip. Then, afraid the nurses would notice something amiss, added, 'Morning, Kay, Jenny. No disasters or major problems I need to know about?'

'A quiet night apart from wee Bee shrieking every now and then.' Jenny handed a file to

Mario. 'When Jackson couldn't get hold of you he talked to Mathew about upping the painkillers. That seemed to work. She settled down quickly.'

Guilt flickered through Mario's eyes. 'Sorry, I must've turned my phone off by mistake. It won't happen again, I promise.'

'No.' Alex almost screamed the word. 'You're not on call 24/7, Mario. None of us are.' This could put a stop to their affair before it really got going.

A loving look caressed her. 'It's okay. We both know that's not true. Being available at all hours comes with the job description of paediatrician. But—' his shoulders rolled eloquently '—occasionally we miss a call and the staff will call on others.' His eyelid dropped ever so slightly. A near wink. 'That's good for Jackson and the other doctors. Keeps them on their toes knowing they have to think about the patients without us breathing down their necks all the time.'

Phew. The affair was still on, then. And her patients were still in the best of care because Mario was right. They had a very good team here, a team that consisted of more than just her and Mario. 'You're right.'

The phone on the nurses' desk rang. 'For you.' Jenny handed it to Mario, who took it and wandered out of hearing. But not out of sight.

'I need Mario to take a look at Bee. Something's not right with her breathing.'

Alex almost leapt off the floor at Jackson's loud voice behind her. 'Mario's busy. I'll come.' Turning, she stared at the intern as though she'd never seen him before. Looking past him she noticed the sunlight falling on the floor at the far end of the ward. Did it always do that? Or just today?

'Bee's coughing badly, and her temp is creeping up again.' Jackson rattled off more details, totally unaware of the way Alex was seeing the world this morning. 'I'm worried.'

A quick shake of her head got her back on track. Until Mario gave her another semi-wink as he listened to his caller, and her heart did that rollover movement again. This was so much harder than she'd have thought it would be. Right now all she wanted to do was drag him into the nearest cupboard and have her wicked way with him.

Which was so unprofessional it shocked her into the real world and had her moving fast towards Bee's room.

'I'm right with you.'

Rochelle was wiping Bee's face and talking sweet nothings to the distressed child.

'You'll make a great mum one day,' Alex told her as she reached for Bee's charts and was astonished at the fiery red stain creeping up Rochelle's neck. Uh-oh. Was she about to lose another staff member to pregnancy?

One day it will be your turn.

The chart clattered to the floor. What? She glanced around the room to see who'd said that but everyone was totally focused on Bee. So her brain was playing cruel tricks on her now. Well, newsflash. She might be embarking on an affair with Mario but nothing else had changed. No children, ever.

Snatching up the charts Alex quickly perused all the obs from throughout the night. 'Take bloods for a CBC, ESR, LFTs and cardiac enzymes. That infection's still not responding to the drugs, and I need to know why.' Moving around the bed she squatted down and spoke softly. 'Bee, is your chest hurting today?'

Alex didn't like the grey pallor of the child's face. Immediately she reached for Bee's wrist, felt for a pulse. More erratic than normal, and far too fast.

'Hurts here.' Bee tapped the centre of her chest. 'And here.' Her small fingers walked over her upper body as she struggled to drag air into her lungs. 'Mummy.' Her lips wobbled and tears spilled down her face into the pillow. 'I want Mummy.'

Just then Jill Sawyer slid into the room and hovered in the background, her face as pale as her daughter's, her arms folded under her breasts with her hands gripping her elbows. 'What's going on? Is Bee all right?'

'I'm giving her a thorough check over, Jill.' No, Bee was not all right, at all. She was in danger of a cardiac arrest. 'Jackson, the defibrilator. Now. Grab Mario while you're at it.' She spoke softly, calmly, in direct opposite to the panic making her own heart race and blood pound. Jackson understood the urgency instantly and dashed off to get the crash cart. No need to hit the emergency button, she had on hand all the staff she needed. 'Rochelle, I need a BP reading.' *Please don't arrest. Please don't. I hate this. I know I can save you if it's at all possible—but what if I don't? What if I fail?* She flicked a fast glance at Jill, saw the terror in her face.

Digging deep within Alex focused entirely on Bee and her obs, watching, waiting, begging whatever and whoever to keep this child safe. Where was that crash cart?

Jackson burst into the room, the trolley with him. Mario ran beside him, quickly followed by Kay. Within moments they had the pads stuck on Bee's chest, the cables snaking over the white sheets to the machine that'd monitor her for as long as it took for her heart to settle back into a more normal state. The machine began printing the graph on her heart rhythm.

Mario called calmly, 'She's gone flat. She's arresting.'

Immediately Alex was on the bed, her interlaced hands pressing down, lifting, pressing, lifting, pressing. Alex didn't take her eyes off the monitor, pleading with it to show a heartbeat. 'Come on, Bee, you can do this. You have to do this,' she whispered, more to herself than the child.

Beside her Mario drew up the drug that would hopefully stimulate Bee's heart, checked it with Jackson before plunging the needle into the girl.

'Bee,' Jill shrieked. 'Beatrice.'

Alex chilled, but she didn't stop the compressions. Her stomach knotted, but her eyes were glued to the screen. *Come on, kid, come on.*

'We've got something,' Rochelle spoke into the tense silence.

'Stop compressions, Alexandra.' Mario tapped the back of her hands.

She knew to do that. But the need to keep this wee heart beating was strong. Slowly, reluctantly, she lifted her hands away from Bee's tiny chest. But she couldn't move too far away. She had to be ready for an instant replay if that little heart stopped again.

A hand on her shoulder, familiar fingers pressing her gently. 'That was amazing. You undoubtedly saved Bee's life.' Mario's voice was full of admiration.

Shudders wracked her. They'd been lucky. This time. They'd done their job and this time there'd been the best outcome possible. She could relax.

'Alexandra?' The admiration had changed to concern.

Straightening her shoulders she shrugged his hand away and stood up on wobbly knees. 'I'm fine.' She mightn't have been able to save her son, but she'd saved Jill's daughter.

Jackson was staring at her. 'That was amazing. How did you know Bee's heart was about to stop?'

'I'll run through my observations with you in a minute.' She turned to the woman standing dumbstruck at the end of the bed, her eyes popping out of their sockets as she stared at her beloved daughter. 'Jill, Bee's doing okay. Her heart stopped briefly but it's beating just fine now.' Thank goodness.

Still Jill didn't move. The bed rail was in danger of bending under the pressure of her grip.

Alex suspected it was the only thing keeping her upright.

Moving to drape an arm around the woman's thin shoulders, she squeezed her into a hug. 'Bee's still very sick, Jill, but she's breathing, living. We're going to help her with that breathing problem next.'

Under her arm Jill moved slowly, turned and peered into Alex's eyes. 'It's never-ending. Every time I dare to think she might be recovering she has another setback. It's so hard.'

'I know.' Jill's pain, anguish, even fury at what was happening to her precious child, tore at her. 'Hug her, Jill.'

She didn't need to add 'carefully.' Since Bee had contracted meningitis Jill had had a crash course how to hold her daughter without interfering with the pads, wires and mask that cluttered Bee's body in times like this.

Leaving Mario with Bee, Alex headed to Kay's office and signed off some letters Averill had left for her. Then she went to see Chloe. 'Hey, gorgeous, how're you doing?'

Chloe blinked up at her, her eyes enormous in her small face.

'Good to see you're not so yellow any more. And I hear Mummy's been feeding you. How good is that?'

Sprawled in the chair beside the crib Kevin snored quietly, his exhaustion less obvious in his relaxed state. Chloe might be out of immediate danger now but her parents still took it in turns to be with her every hour, day and night. Things could go wrong even now. But Kevin had gone back to work part-time while Liz had no intention of gracing the paediatric ward for a very long time.

'Chloe's coming along just fine, isn't she?' Mario's arm nudged her, then remained plastered the length of hers.

Warmth stole through Alex at this small intimacy. It made her feel special, alive even. It made her hope and dream that maybe there was someone in this world for her. Someone who'd love and cherish her the way she'd love and cherish him. 'She's coming on in leaps and bounds now. Kevin and Liz are finally starting to relax about the future.'

'It's been a nightmare for them.'

A sigh slipped across her lips. 'Babies really make a family, don't they?'

'*Sì*. Without bambinos you're only a couple, not a family.' Mario's hand turned, his fingers brushed her palm in a gentle gesture. 'Though what that makes a solo dad and one child I'm not sure.'

'You're still a family.' Then found a grin and told him, 'A little lopsided though.'

A low chuckle and, 'Thanks for that.' Then, softly added, 'What about you? Still adamant you don't want children mucking up your life?'

'Of course I am.' But was she? Watching Liz and Kevin willing their daughter to overcome the odds and win had made her wonder if she was wrong to think she'd never get a second chance. Seeing Mario and Sophia together, loving and sharing despite their rocky start, reiterated her doubts. Mario had shown a mixed-up little girl her place in life, in his life, with kindness, patience and, most of all, bucket loads of love. There'd been a time when family had been the most important thing to Alex, but the deaths of her father and her baby had changed all that. She'd begun to believe she wasn't meant to have her own family, that she was meant to help other families, just not hers. And nothing in her life since had altered her thinking, until recently. Until Mario and his little girl.

'You can have both,' Mario continued quietly. 'I do. Most of us do. Though whether I'm a good dad is up for debate.'

Her neck cricked as she looked up at him. 'Hey, you're doing a fabulous job. Sophia's not unhappy. And she's getting all the physical comforts from you any child should have.'

'Apart from all the donated meals, you mean.' The wry smile he gave her showed how incapable he felt.

Her finger traced the smile. 'You wouldn't look good in a red and blue suit with a cape. Take everyone's kindnesses with the grace they're given.'

The tip of his tongue licked her finger, and a

wicked glint lightened that pewter gaze. 'How come you get it so right for me but so wrong for you?'

'That's where you're wrong. I have it exactly right for me. I know the consequences of believing I should have a family.' With that she stepped back, putting a little air between them so he wouldn't feel the shaking of her muscles as she wondered if she'd made a mistake. Wondered if she could have the impossible dream after all—with Mario.

CHAPTER TEN

'ALEXANDRA PRENDERGAST, HOW do you plead? Guilty…?' The judge paused.

Her heart squeezed with pain. *Not again. Please don't do this to me.*

'Or not guilty?'

She couldn't swallow around her dry tongue. The tears oozed from her eyes, slicked down her cheeks to drip off her chin. 'Guilty,' she tried to whisper. *Guilty, guilty, guilty,* her brain yelled, the word reverberating around her skull.

'No, Alexandra, wrong. You're not guilty. You're innocent, remember?' The man standing on the opposite side of the operating theatre table watched her from friendly pewter eyes. 'You would not deliberately let a child die. You'd do everything in your power to save him.'

'How do you know that?'

'Because I know you. You're a very clever doctor. You care, Alexandra. You care. You saved Bee. You've saved plenty of others. Trust me.'

'I want to so much. But—'

'Trust me, Alexandra.' The honeyed tones sounded so familiar. So sure.

Alex's eyes blinked open. Where was she? She stared around the dark room, recognised the quirky black and silver fabric of her bedroom chair, the silver shine from the bedside lamp stand. She gasped. Mario was here? He'd just spoken to her. She fumbled with the bedside light, finally clicked the switch, bringing in soft light to brighten the dark corners. She peered around but she was alone. In her apartment. Her heart slowed.

Mario wasn't here. But he'd just spoken to her, told her he believed in her. He had to be somewhere in the apartment.

Rubbing her forehead her hand came away wet. Oh. She'd had the nightmare.

But what did that have to do with Mario? He's never been in it before, the voice in her head argued.

It was though he wouldn't believe the judge in

her nightmare. Mario seemed think she was a good doctor. What if he was right? What if she really couldn't have done a thing to prevent what happened to Jordan?

Yeah, but he didn't know about Jordan.

Sliding out of bed Alex picked up her robe and headed for the kitchen and a mug of lemon ginger tea. Her hands were surprisingly steady and her stomach calm, considering the nightmare. But it had been different tonight.

The lemon ginger flavours freshened her mouth, soothed her soul. In the lounge she curled up in an armchair beside the big picture window and gazed down on the quiet harbour. Her eyes followed the headlight on the lone forklift moving meticulously yet quickly between ship and pen, carrying logs that were on the way to China.

To think she'd spent all these years keeping the facts surrounding Jordan's stillbirth hidden in that dark place inside her, not telling people she met that she'd even had a baby. She felt as though she'd cracked wide open and in doing so had reconstructed the facts into a more tolerable scenario. Not that her guilt had vanished. It probably never would, but suddenly she knew she could live with it.

She drained her mug and headed to the smallest bedroom in her apartment. On the art board Harry and Bella were in the middle of a go-kart race, Bella nudging Harry's cart to shove him off the track. Settling comfortably before the board Alex picked up a red pencil and began outlining the 'finish' flag.

Next, with a dark blue shade, she added into the background a small version of a large man with a heart-melting smile. Added his little dark-haired daughter. Then put in another child, a wee boy. Hers and Mario's? The pencil snapped in her fingers. Crazy. She did not, must not, think of having a child with Mario.

But she could continue to enjoy their affair.

Mario felt little fingers poking his cheek and groaned. 'Sophia, Daddy's asleep, darling.'

'No, he's not. He's talking to me.' A giggle followed. 'Come on, Daddy, get up. I'm hungry.'

He made a snoring noise and more giggles filled the room, then little fingers tickled his chin and neck. *Let me catch up on the hours of sleep I missed while making out with Alexandra.*

'Get up, lazybones.' The bedcovers were lifted and a freezing cold foot slid down Mario's belly.

No rest for the wicked or overworked fathers. 'Ahhhh,' he cried, and sat up, scooping his wriggling daughter into his arms. 'Where have you had those feet, missy? In the deep freeze?'

Thank goodness he'd remembered to pull on some pyjama bottoms after Alexandra left in the wee hours. A yawn ripped his mouth wide. When was the last time he'd had so much exercise? Every muscle he had ached or twanged when he moved. But damn, he felt good. The weeks since they'd agreed to an affair had flown by.

'No, Daddy, that's silly. You told me never to open the freezer in case the lid goes bang on my head.'

'So I did. Now what do you want for breakfast, little Miss Muffet? Toast?'

Sophia moved her head slowly from side to side.

'Cereal?'

More sideways moves.

'Eggs?'

'No.'

Mario gave a deliberately big sigh. 'I'm all out of ideas.'

'Daddy, you aren't. There's one more.'

He scratched his chin. 'Umm, let me think. I suppose I could make pancakes with maple syrup.'

'Yes, Daddy, yes, yes, yes.' Sophia clapped her hands so close to his face his nose was in danger of being squashed. Then she leaned forward and placed a sloppy kiss on his jaw. 'I love you, Daddy.'

His eyes misted as his heart slowed and a sweet warmth stole from his head to his toes. '*Sì*, I love you too, sweetheart.' This was what made parenting so special and made up for the frightening moments.

This was why he could only have an affair with Alexandra. There wasn't room for two all-consuming females in his life.

But as he poured batter into the hot pan coated with sizzling butter he wondered if he was being hasty with that decision. Could he have Sophia *and* Alexandra? And more bambinos? Little Alexandra lookalikes running around the backyard? Sophia being the big sister would be squabbling with them. He could hear the racket now. Italian noise, Alexandra would call it.

And despite the number of times he used to hide from his sisters for some peace and quiet as they were growing up, he knew deep down he really wanted this. There wouldn't be much time for paediatrics. Families were all-consuming, especially of time and attention.

But there'd be two paediatricians in the household. They could job share.

Steady up, boyo. You're getting way ahead of yourself. Alexandra has categorically denied wanting to get involved on a deeper level. Not once has she admitted to wanting a child of her own. Though he never quite believed her on that score.

She was so loving, caring. Look how good she was with the little ones on the ward. Didn't mean she'd be keen on being a mother though. But she was great with Sophia. What about those books written and illustrated for children? Surely anyone who did all that wanted to be a mum? She'd loved her father a lot, still felt the pain of losing him. Maybe that was why she didn't want to settle down? Nah, not a good enough reason. A lot of people lost a parent when they were young and went on to have their own family.

He flipped the pancake. If only she'd talk about her past, open up to him. Trust him.

'Daddy, the pancake stinks.' Sophia stood at his elbow.

Yuk. Rancid burnt butter was not a great start to the day. 'Okay, kiddo, Daddy needs to start again.' And needs to stop daydreaming the impossible dream.

Which is?

A more permanent relationship with Alexandra. *Because I can't see I'll ever let her go. I can't get enough of her. She's amazing, and fun, and serious, and so, so addictive.*

Alex stretched her toes towards the end of the bed, her arms above her head. 'I feel so good. You manage to make my body ache in the most delicious ways in places I'd forgotten I had.'

Mario smiled a slow, lazy smile filled with wickedness and a hint of arrogance. 'Glad to know I haven't lost my touch,' he purred.

'Your ego certainly doesn't need boosting.'

They'd come back to her apartment at the end of a particularly gruelling day on the ward with the intention of having a meal. Except neither of them had been anywhere near the kitchen in the hour they'd been here. The moment her door lock clicked shut behind them Mario had hauled her into his arms and carried her to the bedroom. Alex had nuzzled in against his chest, her lips trailing kisses up his neck to his ear where her teeth nipped his earlobe, sending Mario into a hot frenzy.

It had been another beautiful, exciting love-making session. Almost as though they couldn't have enough of each other, no matter how often they got together. The storm was not abating.

Mario reached for the bedside light, and golden light flooded the room.

Alex snatched at the sheet to tug it over her body, but most of it was tucked beneath Mario and didn't come free. 'Hey, roll over, let me have the sheet back.' She nudged him with an elbow. 'Come on, Mario, move.' She had to cover up. Now. Before he saw. Her heart began to speed up and she breathed quick, short gasps. 'Please.'

'Why? You never let me see you fully naked. We've made love in all sorts of positions and yet you're shy of showing me your beautiful body. I don't understand.' Mario raised himself onto an elbow and looked at her, his gaze sliding down her throat to her breasts, down her stomach to the triangle at the junction of her legs.

Alex held her breath. Maybe he hadn't noticed. Please.

His eyes moved down her legs.

She tugged at the sheet again. 'Please, you're making me feel uncomfortable.' In any other situation that languid gaze would've turned her on instantly. But not now. She made to flip onto her tummy.

He reached a hand to stop her, spread his fingers over her belly, his forefinger tracing the telltale lines marring her skin. 'You've got stretch marks.'

Her lip hurt when she bit down. Staring at

Mario she willed him to look away, or meet her eyes full-on so he could see the warning to stop right there. 'Yes,' she whispered.

'You've had a baby.' His hand jerked away from her as though she burnt him and finally he looked directly at her. What Alex saw in those usually sparkling grey eyes turned her cold. Fury, disappointment, hurt—all lashed at her.

Unable to face him from this position she shot out of bed and hauled on the robe lying over the chair. Then she sat on the chair, tucking her feet beneath her. 'Yes, I have.'

'When?'

'Almost ten years ago. When I was twenty-four.'

He latched on to one thing. 'Ten years ago? That's an excuse for not telling me?' He stood and shoved his legs into his trousers, tugged the zip up with such force it was a wonder it didn't jam. His hands slapped onto his hips. 'Were you ever going to mention this? What else haven't you told me?'

Anger at his unforgiving attitude stiffened her spine, tugged her shoulders back. 'We're having an affair, not making a lifelong commitment. That means we don't share all the details of our pasts. Anyway, when we're together we're too busy making love to be talking about all the minutiae surrounding ourselves.'

'Aren't I entitled to know the real Alexandra?' Hurt won over the other emotions darkening his eyes, but he still snapped at her, 'Where is your child? With its father? In Nelson? Or have you left it in another city?'

As Lucy had done. He didn't have to enunciate the words, they were there, hanging in the air between them. The ache in Alex's chest tightened, made breathing difficult as he continued berating her over something that had absolutely nothing to do with him. It was in the past. Her past.

Finally he shut up and she snapped back, 'Thanks for the vote of confidence. You're pretty quick to think the worst of me.'

'Not once have you mentioned visiting a child.' His fingers were white where they gripped his hips. 'Did you have a boy or a girl, Alexandra?'

'A boy, Jordan.' At the mention of her baby's name pain lanced her, sliced her up inside. It

didn't matter how long ago it had happened because at times like this it felt like yesterday.

'And?'

She did not want to talk about Jordan. Not now
when he was so angry. Definitely not when he believed she was capable of the appalling act of de-
serting her baby. Not even his history with Lucy
was an excuse. Besides, why tell Mario when
they weren't in this for the long haul? Judging by
his anger their affair was already over anyway.

'Didn't you love Jordan enough to keep him?
Did you hand him over to his father and get on
with your amazing career?'

She had to say it, shout it at him so he heard
her correctly. 'I am not Lucy. I would never, ever
hand my child over to someone else to raise. Not
even his father. If I'd had to quit med school and
work in a supermarket to support Jordan I'd have
done it.' She leapt off the chair and marched over
to him, stabbed his chest hard with a finger as
the dam burst and the words she'd buried so long
ago spewed forth. 'I would've done absolutely
anything for my baby.' Stab. 'But—' stab '—I
didn't get the chance.' Stab. 'He died. Stillborn.'

She saw the shock jolt through him. 'Alexandra.' He hesitated. Remorseful? 'I'm so sorry. I never expected that, but if you'd told me I'd not have put my foot in it.'

Definitely not remorseful enough. And now that she'd started talking about Jordan she couldn't stop. Mario would get what he wanted—all the details. 'Jordan never once heard my voice. Or got to know my touch. Or to open his eyes and see me. He never felt my love.' She ignored the tears pouring down her cheeks as she bounced on her toes, impaling him with her anger at his criticism. 'I loved my baby. I love him still. I live with this every single day. I see boys of nine and wonder what Jordan would look like now, what he'd be up to, would he love me as much as I love him. I wonder what he wants to be when he grows up. Will he be short like me or tall like his father?' The breaths over her lips were hot, short.

Her hands clenched as she struggled for control. Sinking down onto her heels she took a long, shaky breath and said quietly, 'There you have it. I don't talk about him—to anyone. He's mine.'

Then she turned and walked out of the room,

leaving Mario standing in the middle of her bed-room staring after her. She was done with him. For good. There was no place in her life, in her heart, for a man who didn't listen first, speak second.

In the kitchen she plugged in the kettle and dropped a tea bag into a mug. Her hands shook, her stomach churned and the tears continued.

'Alexandra.' Mario's shirt hung out over his trousers, his jacket crushed in his hand. 'I'm very sorry about your loss. I can't begin to know what you've been through.'

When she didn't say a word, didn't turn around, he said, 'I'll see myself out.'

It seemed forever before the door quietly clicked shut behind him. Alex dropped her chin onto her chest and let go the huge sobs pushing to be freed. Her lungs hurt and her throat ached as her body was wracked with the familiar pain and anger. Only this time the anger was directed at Mario. Blast the man for his accusations. He worked with sick children day in, day out. Why hadn't it occurred to him there might be a very good reason she didn't have her child growing up with her? How could he have thought so little of her?

Just as well she'd learned how judgemental he could be before she made some stupid mistake like thinking their affair could become something more, could flower into the love she'd been starting to hope for. Her hands gripped the edge of the bench to hold her upright. Why did the pain of losing Jordan never lessen? Why tonight did it seem even worse than usual?

Because Mario had accused her of being a bad mother. She might think that but he had no right to. How could he even consider it? Just because that Lucy woman had done something terrible to him and Sophia didn't mean every woman he came in contact with would deliberately mislead him.

Didn't he understand how hard it was for her to talk about Jordan? Her family and friends had known what happened. Those friends had been there for her as she fell apart after Jordan died. They'd supported her when Jonty left. They were the ones to help her get herself back together into someone barely resembling the girl she'd used to be. Nowadays those friends either didn't recognise her or said she'd changed so much they didn't connect with her any more. Why wouldn't she have? Who stayed whole and fun-loving and exuberant when their heart had been chopped out? She'd lost more than her son. She'd lost her husband, friendships, her sense of achievement. She'd become driven, always trying to prove to herself and everyone else she could succeed at everything she tried. Except keep her baby alive.

And now Mario had the pip because she hadn't told him. No wonder she stayed single. If a man couldn't give her unconditional understanding, then she was better off without him. Mindblowing sex or not.

Love him or not.

Mario drove slowly through the quiet streets trying to absorb what had happened back at Alexandra's. Not once had he suspected she was hiding something from him. Not once. When she'd covered her body during their lovemaking he'd put it down to unexpected shyness.

Those few stretch marks had tipped him upside down, shocked him. A trillion questions had rampaged through his skull, all needing immediate answers. Yet he'd failed her in his approach, stamping into the fray like an irate elephant.

How had she coped with the loss? Not very well if the way she slowly dissolved into heart-wrenching tears earlier was anything to go. She'd looked so lost. In agony. Those silent tears streaming down her face as she poked his chest broke him up inside. He'd wanted to haul her into his arms and kiss her better. But he knew how impossible that was. There was no making the situation better. He needed complete and utter trust in a relationship. He needed all the facts laid out right from the beginning. He loathed unexpected surprises.

He turned into his driveway and parked. Next door Gina's house was in darkness. Half an hour of idle chatter would've distracted him. Maybe instead he'd go inside and lift Sophia out of bed and into his arms to hug her close. Just because he could. Too bad that the nanny would growl at him. Because Sophia was the world to him and the reason he hadn't been able to take Alexandra in his arms after her revelation.

So what if he'd been getting closer to Alexandra? Thinking they might take the relationship further into something permanent? He'd been making a mistake and this had been a wake-up call.

Pushing out of the car he headed inside, still pondering why Alexandra hadn't told him about Jordan. She'd had the perfect opportunity when he'd talked about Lucy's treachery, or when he'd asked if she wanted children. It didn't matter to him that Alexandra had had a baby, just that she hadn't told him. She knew how hard it was for him to trust a woman.

Inside he peeked in on Sophia, resisting hugging her, then headed for the liquor cabinet to pour a heavy slug of whiskey. Adding a splash of water he took a deep swallow, let the fire water burn down his throat. Then he sprawled over the couch. It was going to be a long night.

He'd had a few of those lately—with Alexandra. Hot, sexy nights; fun, sleepless nights. Now the affair was over. He could see his sister's disappointment already. She'd thought he might be getting serious about that lovely paediatrician who wrote those beautiful books about the dogs that Sophia adored.

'Tough. This is me looking out for my heart.'

Which didn't seem so clever right this moment.

CHAPTER ELEVEN

WHEN ALEX GOT a break between surgery and the diabetes clinic she popped along to see her favourite patient.

'Hello, Chloe, how's things with you today?'

'I'm doing just fine, thanks,' Liz answered in a cheeky voice.

'Hey, I thought you'd gone home.' Alex crossed to give Liz a hug.

'It's missy's lunchtime. Or should that be second lunch? Now she's started breast feeding there's no stopping her. She's constantly hungry.' Liz looked thoroughly pleased with her daughter.

'You're looking so much more relaxed these days. Positively smug at times.' Motherhood was suiting her friend, especially now that Chloe was improving every day.

Liz's smile slipped, showing how precarious her newfound happiness really was. 'I still wake up at night terrified Chloe's going to develop more problems. I can't believe how lucky we've been.' Another hug. 'You've been wonderful. You and Mario are the best. Best paeds, best friends. I'm meant to wait until Kevin's here to ask this but I can't. We want you two to be Chloe's godparents.'

A lump blocked Alex's throat preventing her from replying. All she could do was nod, and slash at the tears blurring her vision. What an honour. Did Liz know what she was asking? Her, Alexandra Prendergast, to be a godmother to their precious daughter? What if history kicked in? Took Chloe away? She'd never cope with that. Alex wandered to the crib, stared down at the tiny but growing, pink-skinned girl who'd been born fighting. Not once had she given up, no matter what nature had thrown at her. A wacky heart, high bilirubin, lung infection after lung infection, no hugs and kisses from her mum or dad for weeks. A tough cookie who wasn't letting anything stop her from growing and getting healthy.

Learn from her, Alex. Learn from your god-daughter.

'Alex, say something. Have I asked too much of you?' Liz sounded perplexed, as well she might.

Turning, Alex grasped her friend's hands. 'No, you haven't. I'm thrilled, really thrilled. And I swear I'm going to do everything within my power to be the best godmother on the planet.' The tears spilled and poured down her face, and she didn't care. Liz and Kevin believed in her, so why shouldn't she begin to believe she was capable of what they'd asked her to do?

'I've watched you with Sophia. You're so good, so understanding of her. You're a natural with children.'

Hadn't Mario told her the same thing a few days ago when they were still on good terms? Her spine clicked when she straightened her shoulders. Time to start believing everyone and put the past behind her.

Liz asked, 'Is Mario staying in Wellington tonight? I know Kevin's going to want to ask him to be godfather now that I've spilled the beans with you.'

'I think he's flying back as soon as the conference winds up. He doesn't like to be away from Sophia any longer than necessary.' Since their bust-up she'd spent her days trying to avoid Mario on the ward, only getting together to discuss patients and then usually with other staff members close by. But today when she could relax knowing he was out of town she found herself looking for him at every turn. She missed him. Face it, she missed him even when he was here. It was his embraces, his kisses, quick wit and laughter that she missed. Now all she got was a grim countenance.

'Mario probably won't come in here tonight. Kevin might have to pay him a visit at home. If he's not interrupting anything between you, of course.' Liz's wink went straight to Alex's tummy, twisting like a sharp knife.

If only there was something to interrupt. 'Not a problem. I'll be at my apartment.' Where not even Harry and Bella's antics were a distraction any more.

'Is something wrong, Alex? I've just realised

you haven't been as cheerful these past days. I'm
sorry, I've been so tied up in my own problems.'

Alex's pager squawked. Saved. Snatching the
pager from her belt she read the message with a
sinking heart. 'I'm really sorry, Liz. I've got to
go.'

She tore down the ward to the newest patient.
Her heart pounded hard and heavy against her
ribs. Her hands were clammy. A dull ache set up
behind her eyes. She fired questions at anyone
who'd answer them. 'What's happened? How did
Sophia break her collarbone and arm? Has Mario
been told? Is her asthma under control?'

'Mario's cell phone is switched off,' Jackson
replied. 'Not sure if that means he's already flying home or still in the auditorium. Probably the
latter. I think his flight leaves Wellington around
five. I left a brief message which hopefully won't
freak him out.'

'Sophia fell out of a tree,' Kay told her. 'X-ray
shows greenstick fractures of the left ulna and
clavicle.'

'Sophia's wheezing is mild to moderate but is
getting worse as her distress grows. She needs

Mario right now, not in a few hours.' Jackson strode along beside her, ushering her into a side room where she heard loud shrieks coming from. 'In here.'

Alex felt her heart squeeze tight when she saw Sophia, white with pain, her eyes wide and filled with fear while fat tears slid down her face. When she drew a breath the wheeze was obvious. Alex hurried to the bed and sat down. 'Hey, Sophia, I'm here to make you better, sweetheart.' She reached for Sophia, carefully wrapping an arm around her waist, avoiding causing any more pain. 'Shh, sweetheart. It's all right. I'm here.' She kissed the damp curls, rubbed Sophia's back.

'Wh-where's Daddy? I want my daddy.'

'I know you do. Daddy's coming as soon as the aeroplane can get him here.' Mentally she crossed her fingers. 'Do you want me to stay with you?'

The biggest, saddest eyes studied Alex, wrenching her heart again. 'Yes. And Daddy.'

Another kiss and Alex asked Kay, 'Is Gina in the hospital?'

'She's had to go pick up her boys from school. One of them got into a fight,' Kay told her.

Jackson grimaced. 'The youngest has been getting bullied lately so I imagine one of his brothers has stuck up for him again. As if Gina hasn't got enough to deal with.'

So it was true Jackson was seeing Gina out of work. 'Did Gina bypass ED when she brought Sophia in?'

'Hope you don't mind? She figured Sophia would be more comfortable with us than strangers.' Alex liked the protectiveness for Gina sparking back at her from Jackson's eyes.

'I'd have been upset if she hadn't. How long since you put a cast on?'

'Last year during my ED rotation.'

'Right, let's sort out pain control and get our girl fixed up. That shoulder will hurt but hopefully with a soft strapping Sophia won't move it around too much while it heals.'

Jackson's eyes rolled. 'This is a child you're talking about.'

'Wishful thinking, huh?'

'Definitely.' Jackson chuckled. 'Her cousins don't stop moving even in their sleep.'

'I think those boys probably don't have half of Sophia's hang-ups.'

Jackson shook his head at her. 'Their biggest hang-up is when the next meal is due.'

Alex smiled for the first time in days. She'd always got on with Jackson. Maybe because he'd started his medical training in his mid-twenties so didn't have all those hang-ups the junior doctors usually had. 'Sophia, I'm going to give you something to make your arm stop hurting, sweetheart.'

'Where's Daddy?'

'Coming, sweetheart.' She might've spent the past ten days avoiding him but she'd do anything to have him walk through the door right now. 'How about you sit on my knees while Jackson and Kay fix you up?'

Sophia nodded slowly, her thumb back in her mouth.

Half an hour later Sophia's arm was in plaster, her shoulder strapped and her breathing settling down with the aid of her inhaler. She lay curled up on her good side, a thumb in her mouth, and sound asleep.

Beside her bed Gina kept watch over her niece. 'I can't believe she's so settled. Nothing like her last admittance, is it?'

'A fracture isn't as frightening as not being able to breathe.' Alex ran a hand over Sophia's curls.

'More like something to do with her doctor.' Gina grinned. 'She's always at ease around you.'

Alex could feel her chest expanding. Mother material after all?

Gina scowled at her. 'What's up with you and that numbskull brother of mine? He's such a grouch at the moment.'

The air oozed out of her lungs. 'He'll come right. I'm sure it's only a temporary aberration.' But he wouldn't be coming around to her apartment any more.

Gina's scowl softened. 'Don't let him push you around. He's so used to females doing his bidding that if you've stood up to him he'll be in shock.'

'I'll remember that.' Not that she'd have the chance to stand up to him again. At least not in their personal life.

Thankfully Gina let the subject drop. 'I'll have

to leave at five to pick up the boys from my neigh-bour. Think Sophia will be all right on her own?'

Alex smiled. 'I'll sit with her until Mario gets here.' One look at the gorgeous sleeping bundle beside her and she knew wild horses couldn't keep her away.

Gina looked thoughtful. 'Have you heard the weather forecast? Apparently it's snowing in Wellington and the airport has been closed for an hour. Mario might not get back until tomorrow.'

'If that happens we'll keep Sophia in so we can monitor that asthma. I'll sit with her through the night.'

'Mario will love you for that.'

Alex's face tightened as she tried not to look too upset. Not likely. He might be grateful, but he wouldn't love her. And that's how it should be. She did not want his love. Right. Tell that to anyone who'd listen. *If you don't want Mario to love you, then why the sleepless nights? Why the churning tummy 24/7? Why the feeling you've let the most important thing ever to happen to you get away?* Spinning away from his sister's all-seeing gaze she muttered, 'I'll be back as soon as possible.'

She headed for her diabetes clinic with more questions than answers popping up in her brain. *Do I really love him? Is that why I feel sick every time I see him first thing in the mornings? Last thing at night? Not to mention all the minutes in between. I love Mario?*

Yes, I think I do.

No. I know I do.

Her head spun and she leaned against the wall to stay upright. *I've missed him ever since he left my apartment that disastrous night but does that mean I love him?*

Yep. Absolutely.

Great. Now I'm in love with a man who'll never look at me again except to wish I'd vanish in a puff of smoke.

A man who strode through her life every day with patient files in his hands, little lives depending on him. A man who had helped her discover her sexuality on a whole new level to anything she'd previously known.

A man she wanted to have children with, spend

her life with, to see out the golden years beside. The man who'd helped banish her insecurities over Jordan.

'Alex, are you all right?'

Mario? She opened her eyes to find Jackson hovering beside her, concern for her in his eyes. Not Mario, then. Disappointed, she dragged herself straight and continued to the lift. 'I'm fine, thank you.'

Jackson wisely kept his mouth shut until they were down at the day ward and settling into their clinic, then he talked about the patients they were about to see which gave Alex the opportunity to get back on track and focus on what mattered— her patients.

At the doorway into Sophia's hospital room Mario stopped his mad dash to his daughter's side. The air whooshed out of his lungs at the beautiful sight in front of him. The tranquil sight.

He'd been in a state of panic for the past six and a half hours as he'd struggled to get home. When he'd learned there'd be no flights out of Wellington before dawn he'd taken a horrendously rough ferry crossing to Picton where he'd hired a car and driven for two hours in pelting rain and buffeting wind, finally reaching Nelson a few minutes before midnight.

Now here he was and there wasn't a sign of chaos or distress. Quite the opposite. His heart rate slowed and his breathing settled to something near normal. Sophia lay sleeping, her thumb jammed in her mouth. Her other hand poked out from the edge of a plaster cast and was tucked carefully into Alexandra's hand.

Alexandra also slept, her head resting on the pillow beside Sophia, her fair hair a sharp contrast to his daughter's dark locks. *Bella*. Lovely. The book they'd been reading lay open on her lap. Both looked completely at ease with each other. The deep lines that had appeared on Alexandra's face these past few days were smoothed out in sleep. Her mouth had softened, her body relaxed.

As for Sophia—who knew what trauma, stress, she'd been through today? It certainly didn't show at the moment. Thanks to Alexandra? Definitely thanks to Alexandra. Sophia didn't cope with being surrounded with strangers at the best of times. Being in hospital and hurting didn't come close to the best of times.

Crossing the room quietly so as not to wake either of his girls, he picked up a chair and placed it on the opposite side of the bed to Alexandra.

He liked that Alexandra had taken care of his daughter while he was out of town. She had in spades what it took to look after Sophia. She only had to read a Harry and Bella story and Sophia was putty in her hand.

Stretching his legs out he tipped his head back and waited for the night to pass. Waited for the questions to stop buzzing through his skull, the 'I told you so's' to stop laughing at him.

He'd made a mistake with Alexandra. She was perfect for him and his daughter. Except for not letting him in, not sharing her past as he had with her.

Like he'd been entirely up front with her from the beginning? He'd explained why Lucy had struggled to fit in with his Italian family in Florence, hadn't he? How he'd never been there for her, to support her, because he'd been too busy furthering his own interests? He hadn't been fair to Alexandra. Not at all. Would she ever let him make it up to her? Would she forgive him? And if she did, where to from there?

The ceiling blurred before his eyes.

The next thing he knew a nurse was taking Sophia's obs and his neck hurt like hell where it had cricked while he slept. And Alexandra was nowhere to be seen.

'Daddy,' Sophia shrieked, no doubt waking the whole hospital. 'You're here.'

'Hey, gorgeous, how's my girl?' He reached for her warm little body and hugged gently, careful not to bump the damaged shoulder or arm.

'I fell out of the tree in Auntie Gina's yard. The ground broke my arm.' She proudly held up the plaster-encased limb. 'See, Daddy? Alex wrote her name on it. And those are kisses there.' She touched the inky Xs. 'Alex read me a story, a Harry and Bella story so I could fall asleep.' Sophia looked around the room. 'Where is she?'

'She's probably gone home, *amore mio*.' His heart was heavy. 'It's Saturday and Alexandra doesn't always work all day during the weekend.' She'd gone quietly some time while he'd been dozing. Didn't want to wake him? Because she couldn't abide their cold war? It wasn't a war but it sure felt like it at times. Over the past week he'd missed their easy camaraderie on the ward or at their discussions about difficult patient diagnoses or treatment. He'd missed their intimate evenings, stolen hours from hectic lives.

Better get used to it. Nothing has changed. He still couldn't trust Alexandra to tell him the important things in her life.

'Daddy?'

'Yes, sweetheart.'

'Why haven't I got a mummy? Everyone else has.'

So much for thinking he had all the answers.

The storm that had forced Mario to find another way back from Wellington the night before had passed through and the morning sparkled in the early-spring sun.

Dressed in her one pair of jeans, a sky-blue shirt and a thick navy blue jacket Alex strolled through the Saturday market buying fresh salad vegetables. She bumped and jostled with other shoppers, enjoying the slow meander through the crowd. It seemed the fine weather had brought out half the population of Nelson and, though it was nearing midday, the stall holders were still doing a brisk trade.

Daffodils. Her favourite flower. The yellow heads, bright and cheerful, filled rows of plastic buckets at many stalls. She bought six bunches and continued down the row to stop at a stall selling local cheeses where she selected a havarti and a blue. Next to the cheese vendor was the fresh bread man. Choosing a ciabatta loaf she paid and slipped it into her grocery bag along with her other purchases and headed for her car. Hopefully her taste buds would be tempted. Her clothes were beginning to look baggy.

Driving around the waterfront she noted that the clouds had pulled back from Mount Arthur leaving its snow-covered peak glistening where the sun kissed it. 'An absolutely beautiful day.' Amazing how the weather never let her down on this particular day of the year, not once over the past nine years.

Half an hour later she pulled up outside her beach house and turned the engine off. As the roar died away she just sat, gazing down the lawn, over the sand and across the water. The sea was tossing up tiny whitecaps as it did a jittery dance across the bay. Still rough from the storm but not intimidating. Perfect.

'Hello, Jordan,' she whispered. And sat, looking, seeing, remembering.

Finally she pushed open the door and scrambled out, gathered up her purchases and the bag she'd brought from home and went inside. It felt oppressive in there so she left everything on the table and went to open the French doors wide, letting the warmth in. Stepping onto the patio she drew a deep breath. And felt him. Remembered holding her baby in her arms. 'Happy birthday, Jordan, love.'

Her feet dragged as she headed down the lawn to the beach where she crossed to the lapping water's edge. She had no idea how long she stood there. The water covered her shoes, soaked the bottom of her jeans, and still she didn't move. Just stood and let her few memories of Jordan flow into her mind. His beautiful little face, his ten fingers and toes, perfectly formed feet. The wrinkled new skin. The baby smell.

Only when she began shivering from the chill in her feet did she walk back up the beach to sit on the sand, her knees drawn up under her chin, her arms wrapped around her legs. And reran the memories. Again and again. It was cathartic.

Gulls swooped and soared, filling the air with their high-pitched cries, fighting over treasures of food they found on the beach. An old fish skeleton, dead cockles, an apple. It was survival of the fittest—or the meanest. Life at its most basic level.

Alex smiled. Despite what day it was. She loved this spot. Her favourite place in the whole wide world, not that she'd seen a lot of the world, but she just knew nowhere would speak to her like this beach where she'd lived through some of the most important, exciting and harrowing times of her life.

She sensed him before she saw or heard him. She didn't turn to look for him, just carried on watching her piece of beach. He squatted beside her, his hands hanging between his knees. He was so big beside her, so strong. But loving? Wishing for it didn't make it real.

She told him, 'I scattered Jordan's ashes here.' It had been the right thing to do at the time and she'd never once regretted it.

'That first time I was here I noticed how you kept glancing across the lawn to the beach as though looking for someone.'

Sensitive? 'Today's his birthday. He'd have been ten.'

They remained quiet for a while, absorbing the sounds of nature, relaxed together for the first time in a while.

Then Mario said quietly, 'You're amazing. It's a hell of a tragedy to cope with.' He sat down on the damp sand beside her, took one of her hands and held it between both his. Caring?

'Sometimes I thought I was going insane with the grief.'

'That's understandable. Can I ask what happened to Jordan's father?'

'He left me within a month of Jordan's birth. It was dreadful during the days leading up to

Jonty's abrupt departure. He had to blame some-one for Jordan's death, and he picked me for that role. I guess Jonty couldn't handle the whole sit-uation but I didn't see it like that at the time. I thought no loved me enough to stay around.' She shivered. 'Two years to the day I received the di-vorce papers.'

With her free hand Alex scooped up sand, let the grains slip through her fingers. 'We were teenage sweethearts. Met here one summer when he came to stay with relatives. When we were back in Auckland we kept in touch, eventually married and got pregnant.' End of story.

'So you had no one special to help you through your loss.' His thumb rubbed light circles on the back of her hand.

'My mother and stepfather tried, but we'd never had a close relationship and we just couldn't find a connection. I came here for a while because this is where I was happiest with my dad. I'd take long walks along the beach talking to him, cry-ing at the injustice of it all, wishing Jordan back in my arms. I was crazed. It's a wonder the lo-cals didn't have me locked up.'

'They knew you, understood you.'

How did he know that? Because that's how he'd have thought if he'd witnessed a friend going through what she had. He knew stuff like that. She whispered, 'I wish I'd known you back then.'

'You know me now.' Mario slipped an arm around her shoulders and tugged her close, and said nothing. He'd obviously recognised there really wasn't anything more to say.

Loving?

CHAPTER TWELVE

'BIRTHDAYS ARE MEANT to be celebrated. Even Jordan's.' Mario spoke softly, afraid Alexandra might misinterpret his intentions and think he was making light of the situation while all he wanted was to help her through this, to turn the tide against her grief.

Her hand jerked in his grasp. 'No one's ever said that to me before.'

He held his breath.

Scooping up another handful of sand with her free hand she opened her fingers to let the grains dribble through. 'I bought cheese and bread at the market. There's a bottle of wine in the fridge.'

'Then let's have a picnic down here.' Mario stood and reached to pull her to her feet. 'Preferably with chairs so my backside can dry out.'

'Toughen up.' She smiled up at him, sending

his heart rate out of kilter. Maybe there was hope of reconciliation.

How could I have believed I could walk away from her? To have accused her of being as cavalier as Lucy was very wrong. He'd hurt her badly. It had showed in her eyes every time they'd been together at work. He'd had no right to expect her to bare her soul just because they were sharing a bed. There was intimacy and there was intimacy. They hadn't been at the stage where Alexandra felt totally at ease with him. He should've recognised that instead of going off in a funk like a spoilt child. He'd growl at Sophia if she behaved as badly.

Now he understood why Alexandra reacted as she had. That Jonty was a prize bastard. No one deserved to be treated so badly, even if he was also suffering the loss of his son. He should've been sticking to his wife like glue.

As they strolled up the lawn he kept her hand in his, not wanting her to pull away. This was her day and he'd remain with her for as long as she needed him, be strong for her. Did she need him? She definitely needed someone by her side for her son's birthday. Whether he fitted the role was up to her. There was so much love in his heart for her, but he wasn't about to risk the moment telling her. Nor would he apologise for his mistakes. This was her day, not his, not theirs. Right now he was happy to show how much he cared for her.

'Where's Sophia?' she asked suddenly. 'Still in hospital?'

'At home with Gina and the boys. She's not at all distressed about her fall or injuries. Amazing.' Because this woman had formed a bond with Sophia that made her hospital visit a whole lot easier. Sophia liked and trusted Alexandra and he'd do well to follow his daughter's example.

'She feels safe with you now which means the world isn't such a bad place any more.'

Alexandra's certainty unravelled another knot in his gut. He determined to try even harder to make this day work for Alexandra.

Mario put together the picnic while Alexandra went to change out of her wet jeans into a pair of those trackpants she seemed so fond of. He grinned. She was hardly a fashion statement when she shucked off those power suits she wore to work but he wouldn't change that for all the exquisitely dressed women in the world. He loved that she felt comfortable enough in her own skin to dress as she liked, not how she thought the world would want her to.

Sitting on a plastic chair down on the beach Alexandra raised her glass to tap his. 'Thank you. I haven't been on a picnic since I don't know when. Probably right here as a kid with Dad.'

'You've been missing out on so much fun.' Everyone went on picnics. Didn't they?

'My mother and stepfather never had time for such frivolity.'

'Having fun with your children is frivolity?'

'For them it was. Fun was studying music or taking extra lessons so I could top the science class every exam. Not playing.' Her voice petered away and she studied the inside of her glass. 'But I think now that Mother didn't know how to have fun either. Her parents were austere, strict and never laughed.'

'Nothing like you, then. Where did Harry and

Bella come from? They certainly know how to have fun.'

She swilled the wine around the glass, then took a sip. 'I loved art at school. Dad always encouraged me—probably easier on his ears than my singing. In the beginning the stories were my fantasies. They began after Dad died. I guess I was trying to find what I'd lost. Fun, laughter. I'd always wanted a brother or sister to be naughty with, family stuff, you know. Also the dog stories were something that couldn't suddenly be taken from me.'

'Where did your passion for medicine come from?' This was great, learning more about Alexandra in one morning than he had in weeks.

'Dad was a GP and I always wanted to be the same, except I found I loved paediatrics more. Then after Jordan died it became a penance.' She gulped a mouthful of her wine. Swallowing she stared out to sea, seeing who knew what.

'Alexandra, you can't blame yourself for what happened to Jordan.'

'Why not? Jonty did. Jordan was inside me, in my care. No one else's.' She raised a hand, palm out. 'Oh, I know the medical facts, know still-birth happens. But believe me, that counts for nothing when you're the mother.'

'I can see why you'd think that. I really can.' The desolation in her voice had cut him in two. Sometimes his family were overbearing and a right pain in the butt. Sometimes he'd even wished for a quieter life but he'd always known they were all there for him as he was there for them. Alexandra hadn't had that. He refilled her glass and raised it to her lips. 'Thank you for telling me your story.'

'You listened. That's special.' Those beautiful emerald eyes glistened with unshed tears, breaking his heart. 'Since meeting you, seeing you with Sophia, even sharing some time with her, I've started to put my anger and grief aside. I'll always love Jordan, and wish for a different outcome, but I accept now that I can't change that. I'm also beginning to think I might be entitled to a second chance.'

'Of course you are. You deserve it, *tesoro*.' *With me, I hope.* Leaning close he kissed her forehead, her cheeks and finally her lips. Then he pulled back. Now was not the time to take this any further.

Silence fell between them. A comfortable silence nudged occasionally by an errant shrieking gull. The air cooled as the sun descended behind Mount Arthur. The tide began pulling back from its high line.

'Mario, would you stay with me tonight? Here? I need you.' Her cheeks coloured, but her eyes were filled with sadness. And entreaty.

Pushing out of the chair he lifted his Alexandra into his arms and carried her up to the cottage. Tonight he'd look after her, feed her body and soul, make love to her, hold her all night. Today, tonight, forever, he was hers.

Alex woke slowly, opening one eye at a time. She'd slept most of the night. That was a first after a day at the beach with Jordan's memories. Stretching her legs and arms in starfish fashion across the bed she felt the sheets rumpled from making love with Mario, but she didn't come up against the solid warmth of the man who'd chased her bad dreams away.

'Please don't go home. Not yet. Though I did only ask you to stay the night I'm not ready for you to go again.' Staring up at the ceiling where sunlight made patterns from around the edges of her curtains, she smiled.

Last night Mario had been so tender, so generous. His lovemaking had been exquisite. Earlier in the day he'd been caring and sharing and loving. As though he'd forgotten his anger with her, had forgiven her and at the same time accepted he'd been out of line. He'd apologised yesterday. Not with words, but in the hours he'd sat listening to her without trying to suggest she might've got some things wrong, in celebrating Jordan's birthday, and in sharing the night with her.

She needed to hug him, thank him. She needed to tell him she loved him. If he didn't like it, then she'd accept that too. At least she'll have been honest with him.

And nothing ventured, nothing gained. Right?

Mario snapped his phone shut just as Alexandra entered the kitchen, her nose sniffing the air like a retriever. 'Hey, sleepyhead. Thought you'd never wake up.'

'I haven't slept so well in forever.' She headed to the stove top. 'Hot, strong coffee. You're a sweetheart. Exactly what I'm after.' The grin she gave him was big and friendly and happy. 'But first I need you.' Wrapping her arms around his neck she stretched up to plant her mouth on his and as she kissed him she murmured, 'Thank you for everything you did, for being you. You made my day special.'

'I'm glad you let me share it with you. Now, *amore mio*, before you get too cosy I'd better warn you that we are about to be inundated.'

Her eyes popped. 'With Italians?'

'*Sì*, Sophia is fretting a little so I suggested Gina bring her and the boys out here for a few hours. I think Jackson's coming too. Seems he spent the night at Gina's. Sorry to take liberties with your place.'

Alexandra was shaking her head in that sage way she had as she poured coffee into the two mugs he had ready. 'How long have we got alone?'

'Long enough for a shower, not long enough for what you're thinking.' More's the pity.

'Think you're capable of reading my mind now, do you?'

He took the mug she handed him. 'Hell, no. It's shambolic in there. It's the "I want to get laid" look in your eyes that kind of gives you away. You're insatiable.'

Alexandra flicked a tea towel at him, cracking it on his thigh. 'Insatiable, huh? Don't tell me you're complaining.'

'Ouch, and no, definitely not.' Seems their argument was a thing of the past. 'Brunch is coming with the family. Thank goodness, because I've checked out your cupboards and fridge. A man could starve around here, especially after all the exercise I've had. At least the coffee tastes good, even if I say so.'

'I'm taking mine to the bathroom. I'm not greeting all your family in my dressing gown.'

'Or with *I've just had sex* written all over your face.' He laughed as she flicked the tea towel again. 'Careful. I might have to put you over my knee and spank you.'

'Kinky.' Then Alex sucked a lungful. 'Mario, there's something I need to tell you.'

Instantly the laughter died from his eyes, his mouth. 'Yes?'

'I love you.' When he didn't say anything she burbled on. 'I don't know how or when it happened but it's true. I love you. With all my heart. With all me. With—'

His forefinger on her lips stopped the torrent. 'Thank you, *amore mio*. And I love you. I've been busting to tell you. Wanting to shout it out across the beach. But this is your weekend, yours and Jordan's. I didn't want to encroach. But bottom line is I love you.'

Alex thought she'd implode with the love and warmth and excitement and everything she felt for this wonderful man. Her hands met around his neck and she pulled his mouth down to hers. 'To hell with the family. Let's celebrate,' and she tugged him towards the bedroom.

Two hours later Alex stared around her cottage in amazement. Not for a very long time had there been so many people squeezed in here and yet it felt right somehow. Gina and her boys had swarmed in and made themselves totally at home, putting up enough food to feed an orphanage, all laughing and chattering at once so that no one could hear anyone else. Jackson had trailed behind, a bewildered yet happy expression on his face. He was now chasing the boys and Sophia around the lawn accompanied with ear-splitting shrieks filling the bay.

Gina and Mario kicked Alex out of her own kitchen. 'Set the table up on the lawn where it doesn't matter if the bambinos make a mess.'

Gina banged a pan down on a gas ring. 'Oh, and don't forget glasses for the champagne Mario demanded we bring.'

'He did?'

Beside her a deep sexy voice told her, 'What's brunch without champagne?'

'A dry argument?'

'No more arguing for you and me,' he murmured against her neck as his tongue did a little lick thing on her oversensitive skin.

Turning, she slid a hand behind his neck. 'You're right. Been there, done that, and didn't like the consequences. So we're definitely okay again?'

Mario's eyes smouldered back at her, granite coloured. His tongue flicked over his bottom lip. Under her hand he trembled briefly. 'Come with me,' he growled before grabbing her hand and hauling her outside and down to the beach without giving her a chance to answer.

'What happened to you and me cooking brunch?' Gina called after them.

Mario looked around. 'Jackson, you're wanted in the kitchen.'

At the water's edge Mario stopped and turned Alex to look at him, his hands on her waist, a very serious expression on his face. His Adam's apple bobbed. 'Alexandra.' Her name slid off his tongue in her favourite way. Another swallow. 'Alexandra, I screwed up badly. I had no right to demand you tell me such private things about your baby. Not even what Lucy did lets me off the hook. I am very, very sorry for getting so angry.'

'You showed me that yesterday. No one has ever turned Jordan's birthday into a celebration before. That was unbelievably special.' And now she could dream about having more children. But first she had to catch her man. 'Mario—'

His finger pressed her lips. 'Shh. Let me finish. I know I'm rushing things but today seems the perfect day with family here and the cold bottles of champagne waiting to be popped open.' Another swallow and he was saying in his heart-melting voice, 'Alexandra, I love you with all my heart and I want to marry you, have bambinos with you, even retire and race mobility scooters with you in the distant future.'

Laughter vied with tears as she reached her hands to his face to pull him down and kiss him. 'Yes, yes, yes. I love you so much I'd do anything to be with you for the rest of our lives. Even fine-tune your engine.'

'You certainly know how to keep that running.'

'Right.' She covered his mouth with hers, then pulled back. 'I think I've loved you from the moment you strode through my ward looking like it was yours.' Then before he could argue she kissed him, long and hard.

Cheers and clapping broke their kiss. Alex found herself torn from Mario's arms and embraced by Gina. 'Welcome to the Forelli mob,' her soon-to-be sister-in-law said.

Jackson handed round glasses of champagne to the adults and lemonade to the kids.

'To my beautiful Alexandra, *tesoro*.' Mario held his glass high.

'Daddy, what's happened? Why's everyone laughing?' Sophia appeared at Mario's side and tugged at his hand. 'Why's Alex crying?'

Alex dropped to her knees in the sand and reached a hand to the sweetest little girl she'd ever encountered. 'Sophia, Daddy's asked me to marry him. Is that all right with you?'

Big brown eyes studied her in the sudden silence. 'Are you going to be my mummy?'

'Is that what you want?' Her heart thudded in her ears, because if Sophia said no, then she wasn't marrying Mario. This child had first dibs on him.

'Yes, please, Alex.'

And suddenly Alex was being squashed in a cuddle with her fiancé and daughter-to-be, and more cheers were deafening her as her glass tipped in her hand and spilled its contents over her feet.

Mario whispered, 'Think of all those bambinos we can make.'

Gulp. Her own children. 'Ahh, could we start with just one?'

'Not a problem. I know when you hold our first baby you'll be begging me for more.' His eyes twinkled at her, warming her heart, curling her toes.

'How many grandchildren do your parents think they can handle?'

'Lots.' Mario grinned. 'Be warned. There are days with my family that you'll want to hide in the back of a wardrobe with a torch and a good book.'

'Trying to talk me out of this now?' She couldn't stop smiling, she felt so alive and happy. She had a future to look forward to.

'No, you'll find I'm already in there. I'll bring the cheese and bread, you bring the champagne.'

One year on...

Alex lay back against the pillows on her hospital bed. Her left arm cuddled baby Forelli, female.

Her right arm cuddled baby Forelli, male. Age two hours twenty minutes.

Her face ached from her permanent smile. Her heart throbbed with pride, joy and relief.

Mario and Sophia sat on the end of the bed arguing over the babies' names.

Sophia wanted to call them Harry and Bella.

Mario wanted to call them Alexander and Alexandra.

Alexandra just wanted to hug them all forever. This was her family. Loud, noisy, beautiful.

* * * * *

STIRLING
COUNCIL
LIBRARIES

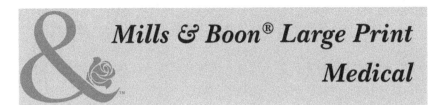

November

December

January

Mills & Boon® Large Print

Medical

February

MIRACLE ON KAIMOTU ISLAND	Marion Lennox
ALWAYS THE HERO	Alison Roberts
THE MAVERICK DOCTOR AND MISS PRIM	Scarlet Wilson
ABOUT THAT NIGHT…	Scarlet Wilson
DARING TO DATE DR CELEBRITY	Emily Forbes
RESISTING THE NEW DOC IN TOWN	Lucy Clark

March

THE WIFE HE NEVER FORGOT	Anne Fraser
THE LONE WOLF'S CRAVING	Tina Beckett
SHELTERED BY HER TOP-NOTCH BOSS	Joanna Neil
RE-AWAKENING HIS SHY NURSE	Annie Claydon
A CHILD TO HEAL THEIR HEARTS	Dianne Drake
SAFE IN HIS HANDS	Amy Ruttan

April

GOLD COAST ANGELS: A DOCTOR'S REDEMPTION	Marion Lennox
GOLD COAST ANGELS: TWO TINY HEARTBEATS	Fiona McArthur
CHRISTMAS MAGIC IN HEATHERDALE	Abigail Gordon
THE MOTHERHOOD MIX-UP	Jennifer Taylor
THE SECRET BETWEEN THEM	Lucy Clark
CRAVING HER ROUGH DIAMOND DOC	Amalie Berlin